WHAT THE BEAR SAID

WHAT THE BEAR SAID

SKALD TALES FROM NEW ICELAND

W.D. VALGARDSON

TURNSTONE PRESS

Turnstone Press
Artspace Building
206-100 Arthur Street
Winnipeg, MB
R3B 1H3 Canada
www.TurnstonePress.com

Turnstone Press gratefully acknowledges the assistance of the Canada Council for the
Arts, the Manitoba Arts Council, the Government of Canada through the Canada
Book Fund, and the Province of Manitoba through the Book Publishing Tax Credit
and the Book Publisher Marketing Assistance Program.

Cover design: Jamis Paulson
Interior design: Sharon Caseburg
Printed and bound in Canada by Friesens for Turnstone Press.

Library and Archives Canada Cataloguing in Publication

Valgardson, W. D.
    What the bear said : skald tales from New Iceland / W.D. Valgardson.

ISBN 978-0-88801-380-4

    I. Title.

PS8593.A53W43 2011   C813'.54   C2011-903242-2

For Janis Olof Magnusson

CONTENTS

From the time I was a small child in Gimli, Manitoba, until the time my parents left their house to go into a nursing home, their kitchen table was a centre for storytelling. The coffee pot was always on. No one knocked on the back door. Visitors from near and far came in already talking. On Sundays, people came and went, with chairs around the table never being empty for long. At the centre of the storytelling were two subjects: one was commercial freshwater fishing in the Interlake area and the other, the Icelandic community in the Interlake and beyond. In those early days, conversations were often in both English and Icelandic. However, even in the 1940s, the Ukrainian settlements west of Gimli were causing a change both in daily life and in storytelling. Intermarriage between the Ukrainians and the Icelanders had been taking place for some time and many of the stories around the kitchen table began to include Ukrainians. Festive meals now had both vinarterta and perogies.

However, Gimli remained very Icelandic. Attitudes and beliefs had been passed down through the local Icelandic-Canadian community. The community celebrated Íslendingadagurinn, the Lutheran church was the centre of much social activity and the local monument to the town's history was to the Icelandic settlers. Stories I heard often had fragments of Icelandic folk tales in them, except none of us knew it. These were like bits of pottery shards, except no one tried to reconstruct the original vessel. The stories of large fish, of terrible storms, of shipwrecks, of life as a fisherman/farmer, were set in New Iceland, but had behind them centuries of storytelling in Iceland. Whether the "other folk," the trolls, giants, *huldufólk*, magical sea creatures, also came to North America with the settlers is still debated. All I can say is their life in the minds of the Icelandic North American community proves to me they did.

The emigration from Iceland was a painful one. People were driven away by hunger, by political oppression, by dire poverty and lack of any hope for the future. As hard as life in Iceland had been, the emigrants, once settled in Canada, were torn by longing for Iceland's landscapes, history, and lost family relationships. They tried to build a New Iceland but their efforts were shattered time and again. They brought with them, though, a love of books and literature, of memories of evenings in the *baðstofa* when stories were told, when *rímur* were sung and books were read aloud. The love of storytelling and poetry continues to this day.

Some stories crossed the ocean largely unaltered, but only small pieces of others survived. I've used Icelandic folk tales as the models for these stories and tried to be as true as possible to the storytelling I heard as a child.

WHAT THE BEAR SAID

WHAT THE BEAR SAID

When the bear first spoke, Gusti was in his skiff lifting a net. The fish were in close to shore that summer and his nets were set perhaps a hundred feet from shore. It was a fine summer's day, the kind of day that made him think he'd been wise to leave Iceland. The memory of the terrible winter was fading. The sun was warm on his back. He could see his cabin and the small barn he'd constructed for his animals. He'd cleared the trees and bush with an axe, then pried out the stumps with an iron bar. He'd tilled the ground with a mattock.

The weather had been warm with just enough rain to help the barley and wheat grow. The potatoes, turnips, and beets were thriving. He could see his three children in the potato patch. They were picking potato beetles off the plants.

He loved his two boys but his daughter, Ninna, was his favourite. Ninna was three. The boys kept an eye on her because, although she was the youngest, she was also the most adventurous. She'd dash off into the bush to look for berries. She'd climb onto the tallest stump and jump off. She also ran to hug Gusti's leg every time he came back home from cutting wood or from town with supplies. When he finished lifting his nets and returned to the cabin, she'd greet him by squealing and holding out her arms so he would pick her up.

He was pulling a fish out of the net when the bear first spoke. It made him stop with a pickerel half out of the mesh. It wasn't as if he'd heard anything through his ears, but more like something had happened inside his head. At least that was what he said when he'd still talk about it.

He broke out of his reverie and looked back to shore. A mother bear and a cub were sitting on the sand. The sow was big, and in the summer sunlight her fur looked brownish red. She was staring intently at him and he was afraid that she might attack. She did not move and he didn't dare risk moving. If she were to charge, he'd never be able to drop the net, sit down, and get the oars into the oarlocks before she'd have raced through the water to him. Bears were great swimmers and she would have ripped the side off the flat-bottomed skiff or climbed over the gunwale, capsizing it before he could escape. He'd have no chance in the water. He'd seen the claws of dead bears, claws as long as his fingers, sharp, curved, made for killing.

He stood absolutely still. Neither Gusti nor the sow moved and then, startled, he thought, she's asking me for fish. The previous winter had been harsh and the spring late. The berry bushes had bloomed, and then frost had killed the blooms. There were few berries that year and there'd been a number of reports of bears attacking cattle. Those that had been shot were thin, their stomachs empty.

Now, when he looked more closely, he could see how gaunt both she and the cub were. In Iceland, he'd seen people and animals thin like that, dumb with hunger, all bones and loose skin, passive, standing or sitting and watching, waiting, hoping that someone would give them something to eat. That was when things were so bad that people were soaking fish bones in *sýra* until they were soft enough to eat.

Here, in New Iceland, no one ate softened fish bones. They threw the bones and guts away, keeping only the livers and the roe.

When Gusti had started fishing, he'd been told by the Indians not to throw the offal into the water because if it washed onto shore it would draw bears. Some people had tried burying the heads and guts but the bears, with their keen sense of smell, dug them up. Normally, Gusti rowed a good distance into the lake and fed the heads and guts to the gulls and pelicans.

The water was flat calm. There was no sound. Neither the bear nor Gusti had moved. Then Gusti nodded. He wasn't sure why he'd nodded but he knew what he had to do when he finished lifting the nets. There was a large rock three fathoms from shore. The top had been smoothed nearly flat by the waves and ice. He rowed his boat up to it, then, as he cleaned the fish, he threw the offal onto the rock. The sow and the cub never moved and the sow never took her eyes off him. When he was finished, he looked up and, for half a minute, they stared across three fathoms of water into each other's eyes. He rinsed his knife before rowing away from the rock. As soon as he'd backed off, the sow waded into the water and the cub followed her. The cub was standing against the rock, trying to get up. She bent down, grabbed it by the back of the neck and lifted it. Together, they ate everything and finished by licking the rock clean.

When he told his wife what happened, she protested, saying that to feed bears was to invite trouble.

"A hungry bear is a dangerous bear," he said. "A full bear will leave our sheep alone."

What he didn't know how to explain was what had happened in his head when the bear had spoken to him. It wasn't like fog. It was more like ink being dropped into water. A sudden blackness, like a dark cloud, spreading and dissipating.

All that summer the bear talked to him. She left him with the memory of swirling dark clouds, a sensation of something primitive, stirring something within him, memories of ancient times, faint images that appeared and faded so quickly he could not really say what he had seen. After he'd left the remains of the fish on the rock a few times, he did not row so far away anymore, but sat so close that the rank smell of the mother and cub reached him. The sow would stop eating from time to time to stare at him but the cub ignored him until the fish were all gone. Gusti left whole fish on the rock now. These were fish he and his family would not eat because they did not have scales. He banged the back of their heads on the gunwale to kill them, then piled them onto the rock. When everything was eaten and the cub was back in the water, the sow would stand, her forepaws on the rock, and look across it, studying him, before shaking herself and plodding to shore.

One day the smell of fish brought a large black bear. The cub was on the rock. The cub's mother turned, stood at her full height and roared. The black bear charged forward. They fought, forelegs locked, each trying for a crippling bite. They broke their hold, then slashed at each other again. Finally, the intruder retreated, sulking on the beach a while before leaving.

While they'd fought, Gusti had poled the skiff forward until it was hard against the rock. If the fight had gone against the sow, he'd been ready to take the cub. Victorious, the sow stood, licking her bleeding shoulder. That was when he heard something, although later, he could not have said exactly what he heard. She stopped licking, turned her head and stared into his face. Ink falling into water, that was the only way he could explain it, but this time turbulent, as if the water were moving and the ink, thick, holding together longer.

"Talking to bears," they said in town, shaking their heads. "What next?" He would not be the first to lose his wits living on a lonely homestead. There were those who'd hung themselves from a crossbeam or walked fully clothed into the swamp.

When Gusti was in town, it was suggested that he borrow a rifle and when the bears came to feed that he shoot them from his boat. He declined. Then it was suggested that if he were afraid that he'd miss and only wound the sow, he should hire someone to do the job for him. He'd have none of it.

"It'll all come to a bad end," Arinbjörn of Borgarfjörður said. He knew about bears. One had killed his best milk cow. He'd hunted it for three days before killing it. Its pelt was now on his cabin floor.

No one, of course, wanted to hear about ink in water. No one wanted to think about what it meant if bears could talk and that, if we listened carefully enough, or if they caught us unexpectedly so our old abilities might reappear, we could understand them. It was easier to be afraid, and fear justifies anything, even killing.

"What do you talk about?" one of the jokers at the Gimli store said. "Do you just pass the time of day? Or do you discuss philosophy?"

"It wasn't like that," Gusti tried to explain. "It was an understanding." The way fishermen in Iceland sometimes talked about the whales that surfaced beside them. Terrifying because they could tip over a boat at will or by accident but, sometimes, swimming around and around the boat as if studying the boat and men.

"This," said Arnibjörn, patting his rifle, "is all bears understand."

It was then that Gusti stopped trying to explain.

The summer waned, the cold weather came, and then it was replaced by Indian summer. The lack of berries had meant an increase in bear attacks on cattle and sheep. Bears had broken into a number of cabins to get at food but Gusti's sheep and cattle went unmolested. Sometimes, at night, he heard a fierce roaring as bears fought nearby. The sow, he thought, protecting her territory.

The snow came. For a time, even when there was a rim of ice on the shore, he fished and the sow and cub still came but, gradually, they came less and less. He realized that he missed them. He missed that odd feeling when both he and the sow were still, watching each other, and something formed in his head, like shadows from a fireplace on a wall. He now watched the tree line as he fished, hoping to see the mother and the cub stroll onto the beach and sit down at the water's edge. When they didn't come, he felt something like grief.

"It is something like a dream," he said to his wife. He grew exasperated with himself. "But not like a dream. As if we have memories from our parents and our grandparents and our great-great-great-grandparents somewhere in the distant past but we don't know we have them and this is stirring them up. What if," he said, "at one time, we could talk to the animals? What if Noah understood them?"

His wife, Vigdís, loved Gusti and she understood that besides being a fisherman and a farmer, he was also a poet. Many a night when he couldn't sleep, he sat at the table, writing poems. He had memorized poems from the *Edda*. In the evenings, he would recite them as they knitted. She also remembered, although she'd never told anyone but Gusti, that, in Iceland, when she'd been caring for the sheep one summer, she'd seen a procession of people who'd disappeared into a cliff. As clear and plain as she'd seen the sheep grazing around her.

One day the children were out gathering wood and a blizzard came out of nowhere. The snow was so thick it was nearly impossible to see. The boys had called to Ninna but the snow muffled all sound. They frantically searched for her. When it began to get dark, they rushed home. The family all went out then to look but the heavy snow had drifted over everything. They dug at every mound. They crossed and re-crossed the area where the children had been collecting wood. Finally, they had to return home. In the darkness and swirling snow any one of them could get lost.

None of them slept. Twice, Gusti and Vigdís tried to go out but there was no moon and the blowing snow was blinding. Although they each carried a lantern, they could see nothing. They were forced back to the cabin by the wind. Ninna's brothers huddled together in their bed and cried.

They waited for dawn. The world was white and silent. They went out again, although now any hope they had of finding Ninna alive was gone. Still, they searched. They each took an area of bush. The sun sparkled on the snow and the snow, as it warmed, fell from the branches of the trees. They called her name and their voices, overlapping, faded and were lost amidst the trees and underbrush. Gusti sent the boys to search the lake. She could have wandered out onto the ice.

It was just a few minutes later that Gusti heard a noise. He stopped. In the silence he could hear the snow creak under his moccasins. "Ninna," he called.

"Here, *Pabbi*," she called back, but there was nothing to see. She called from beneath the earth and he wondered if she called from the grave.

8

"Ninna," he called again and she replied. "Keep calling," he said, "so I can find you."

Each time she called, he moved closer to the sound. There was, he saw, a small opening in the snow. Her voice rose from there. "It's dark," she cried. "Pick me up."

He brushed away the snow. There was a small hole in the snow and when he had cleared enough away, he saw that there was a large hole in the ground. Below him, sunlight fell on an upturned face.

"I fell in," she said matter-of-factly.

He lay on the snow and reached down. She reached up. He grasped her arms and heaved her out of the hole. A rank heavy smell he recognized came up with her.

"A bear's den," he said, when he told people about finding her. "She'd fallen into a bear's winter den."

Gossip was that when the child had been lost and crying, a large brown arm had reached from the den and pulled her down. Others scoffed at this but said only that she'd fallen in and the bear had kept her warm through the long night. Others said that was not true, that there had been no bear because it was an abandoned den.

For the rest of his life he was known as Gusti Bear and his daughter as Ninna Bear. Gusti Bear's homestead prospered. He added a large piece of land, larger than he could ever farm. He kept much of it in bush and as long as he was alive, no one was allowed to hunt bears on his property.

SIGGA'S PRAYER

It could have been the troll woman," Inga said as she worked at the spinning wheel. They were crowded together, sitting on the edge of their beds as they cleaned and carded the wool.

"Almar saw something," Jakob agreed.

They were silent, thinking of what it meant if, after all these years, a troll had returned. Since the farm owner's grandfather, Old Bjarni, had killed a troll on the mountain, there'd been no sign of trolls or their mischief.

The farm had once been plagued by a troll who carried away sheep and even a horse and who, time and again, had tried to lure people up the mountain. To collect sheep on the upper meadows was frightening and few would risk it. When they went there to bring sheep down for the winter, or when they went to collect moss for their winter food supply, they went as a group.

After Old Bjarni had lost three of his prize milking sheep, he said, "This is too much," and, despite everyone warning him against going to challenge the troll, he went to his smithy and turned the short blade of a scythe into a spear. He shaved a piece of driftwood into a handle.

"I would have my ancestors' good weapons, but we have to make do with what we have." He left with the fog swirling around him. He said that he would be back before nightfall because he knew the location of the troll's cave.

Night came early, for summer was over and the days had shortened. They put a lamp in the window so that he might find his way home but he did not appear. Some stayed awake all night, waiting and watching.

Others went to the door and called his name but they heard nothing, neither Old Bjarni's voice, nor the troll hollering. The fog was so thick no one dared go out for fear of becoming lost.

The day passed, and another night; then the fog began to lift and, once again, they could see the fields and the mountain slopes. Nothing moved except sheep here and there.

"I'll find him," said Old Bjarni's son Gréttir. "Who will come with me?"

No one looked at him. Instead, they studied the work they were doing, or their hands, or the sky.

Old Bjarni's grandson, Helgi, was ten. "I'll come," he said. He stepped forward and stood beside his father.

"Those who come with me," Gréttir said, "will get two pieces of fish and a dish of butter."

Hunger can overcome fear and three of the men said they'd go with him but if the troll appeared, they'd not stay to fight it.

There was not much with which to outfit them. Viking swords and shields had long ago rusted away in forgotten graves. They took three sickles and two knives used for butchering sheep.

The way up the mountain was not easy. There was loose sand in which every step meant sliding back half a step. There was sharp lava that could tear off a man's flesh. They picked their way over loose rock and around small waterfalls.

The higher they went, the more nervous the farm workers became. The higher they went, the smaller and less effectual their knives and sickles looked. The troll was large, three times the size of a good-sized man, with broad shoulders and heavy thighs and legs that let him lift large boulders and throw them a great distance. More than one man, travelling by himself, had narrowly escaped a boulder sent crashing down the mountain.

They climbed to the snow line but did not want to go beyond that. None of them had been above where the snow line began because the sheep never went to where there was no grass.

"You've come a long way," Gréttir had said to the three *vinnumenn.* "It would be a shame to lose both fish and butter and a bowl of soup with a piece of fat meat in it because you are afraid of going somewhere you've not gone before."

They had climbed a long time and their hunger was greater than usual. First one crossed into the snow and followed Gréttir and Helgi's footsteps, then the other and, finally, the third, although the third hung back, letting the others get well ahead of him, until he realized if the troll appeared from behind, he'd be the first taken up.

They worked their way around rocks and along shelves until they came to where three ravens were circling.

Here they found Old Bjarni, lying at the entrance to a cave. His spear was broken, the haft splintered. He was lying on his back, his mouth and eyes open, as if he'd seen some unimaginable terror. Beside him was a large stone that might have been a man on his hands and knees with his head between his arms. The wounded troll had been unable to crawl out of the sunlight.

They carried Old Bjarni down, one to each arm, one to each leg. It was a slow procession. When they reached the bog at the foot of the mountain, others came to help and carried him on their shoulders.

They buried him and made a mound over his grave, then covered it with large stones. On each stone, they scratched a cross so no children of the troll could uncover him and drag away his body. They put a wooden cross at his head and when the priest came to test Helgi for his catechism, he also said a prayer for the grandfather's protection because some battles continue even after the contestants have given up their mortal souls.

All had been quiet after that. No more sheep went missing. The cows and sheep gave good milk. When the women went with their tents to pick moss, no one molested them. There had been the weather to contend with, for there had been cold years with ice filling the bays. The cold kept the grass from growing, so every blade was precious. They waded into the bog to reap even a handful of grass. During the winters there had been snow so heavy the men and boys had to clear ground to help the horses reach what little grass there was. The people on the farm ate more Icelandic moss than usual and, in the spring, had come close to boiling their sheepskin clothes and eating them. A gift of warm weather and the return of some swans they'd been able to catch had saved them. Since then, they'd been able to plunder a few nests.

But now that years had passed, and with Gréttir dead, too, the depredations of a troll had begun again. There were two missing sheep. The side of the mountain had fallen, the mud and rocks cascading down, burying a good grass field. Some thought they'd seen a troll high up the slope where the avalanche had started. They feared avalanches. There were places where all the meadows of a farm had been covered by landslides and, in an instant, a farmer was reduced to poverty.

"Perhaps Helgi is unlucky," Inga said as she spun.

They all stopped the carding or weaving or knitting that they were doing. To be born without luck was like being born a cripple. No matter how smart someone was, the wind or the frost could turn against him, the unseen could surprise him at any hour, the mountain could cover his fields so his cattle died of hunger.

They said no more of it, because if Helgi were unlucky, then so were they, for here they lived as servants and welfare cases. There were two *húsmenn* on the farm who were no longer able to go fishing and had to remain behind. The rest were all women and children.

"He needs a wife," Sigga said. She was picking dirt out of the wool.

They all looked at her. She was a strong young woman who knew how to work.

"And who do you think he should marry?" Inga asked slyly.

"Helgi has no luck with women," Jakob said. Jakob made horsehair ropes and was clever at repairing the gear for the horses.

It was true. Helgi had been widowed twice. His first wife had drowned crossing a river and his second, along with their two children, had died of diphtheria.

"If the cod don't come this year—" Sigga said, then stopped. It was on all their minds. It was the lack of dried fish that had them nearly eating their sheepskin shoes. They usually ate wind-dried fish with a bowl of butter. There had been nothing to trade with the Danish merchant ships so there was no rye to grind. None of them had seen bread in a long time. This year there had not even been enough fish heads for boiling.

"No one here died of hunger this winter," Inga replied sharply. She had lived at the farm since she was a child.

It was true. At other farms, many had died. No one had anything to give. Hunger was everywhere.

"Without this pasture—" Jakob said, then bit his lip. They knew the consequences of even the smallest loss of hay. It had been a long time since it had been possible to grow grain. In good years, there was a wild grain they could collect and grind. They could mix it with the moss and make flat cakes. This year, none of the lime grass seed had ripened.

"It is not just Helgi who has no luck," Inga said. She had started a pair of mittens. They could tell she was upset by the way she jerked the needles from time to time.

They hoped Helgi would bring fish piled high on the horses, in great bundles, enough dried fish for a year. Often, they dreamt of fish and what it was like when there was enough for breakfast and supper. But sometimes they dreamt of the fishing, of the boats being pulled into the raging surf and men, burdened down by their sheepskin waterproof clothes, being dragged into the water and drowned. Sometimes, they dreamt of boats foundering in the waves and men thrashing about, unable to swim, disappearing beneath the surface. They were too frightened to talk of these things.

They worried for themselves but they also worried for Helgi, because he was a good man. He treated everyone well. As hard as he worked, Helgi did not have much more than any of his workers. The farm was on the edge of the desert so the land was marginal. The last of the winter was always difficult. They scraped the bottoms of the food barrels but Helgi, even when it meant that he was not full at the end of a meal, took no one else's share.

He beat no one with a rod or tree root. He made certain they all learned to read and write. No children failed their catechism and, when the minister came to test the children's ability to read and recite, Helgi always fed the minister as well as he could.

A traveller who came from the coast stopped briefly at the farm to tell them a boat with fifteen men had capsized and all had drowned, and that a week later another boat of fifteen men had disappeared in a storm. On hearing this, they clutched their hands to their chests, grieving for those who had died but grateful because neither boat had been Helgi's boat. The word was the cod had not come close to shore this year, forcing the fishermen out further into the open sea where the wind and waves made fishing more treacherous than ever.

The traveller had brought a letter from Ameríka for Sigga. Her two brothers had gone to New Iceland on the shore of Lake Winnipeg. They said times were hard but they had enough to eat and had jobs. They included money to pay half her fare to Ameríka. They said they would send the rest as soon as they could. They knew where she could work for board and room and five dollars a month. The food, they said, was good and there was lots of it.

"The wild animals will kill you and eat you," Inga said. Her mouth was a rigid line.

"They haven't killed and eaten my brothers," Sigga replied.

"Iceland needs us," Jakob said. "Soon the Danes will be gone and if young people leave, who will make Iceland great?"

Runa usually said nothing. She was weaving. "Many die on the trip. They are buried at sea."

"Many die here," Sigga answered. "They are buried in the sand."

"Maybe there will be no boats from England this year," Jakob said.

Sigga said no more. She bent over her work, cleaning the wool as she rocked back and forth. She knew they did not approve of people leaving Iceland. As hard as life was, they thought people should stay instead of running away. None of them had more than a quilt, a wooden bowl, a horn spoon and their clothes, but their life was what they knew. She wanted to say to them that it was not just Icelanders leaving. She'd heard that Norwegians were leaving Norway for Ameríka in even greater numbers than Icelanders were leaving Iceland.

The next morning, she went out early. She walked toward the mountain, toward the dark spot where they said the cave of the troll was and, at the edge of the bog, she paused.

Her brother's letter had said there was food and it was good. There was a job that paid money instead of just board and room and two Danish *rigs* dollars a year. Every house had a stove. To marry, a man didn't have to own land. She could have a family. She could save her money and buy a new dress. Letters from Ameríka said you could have a wooden house like the Danes lived in at the Icelandic harbours. She had never seen them, but visitors had told her about them. Wooden houses with stoves, carpets, wooden floors instead of damp dirt, and individual rooms instead of eighteen people sleeping jammed into one room for heat. The houses sounded like the luxurious homes of the *huldufólk*, the hidden people.

She crossed on the tussocks. She began on the sheep path up the mountain, climbing, sometimes crawling, wrapping her wadmal cloak around her against the wind. Her sheepskin slippers were no protection against sharp lava and her feet soon bled. She came to the snow. The cold stopped the bleeding but she left imprints marked with blood. She came, at last, to the cave. She rested just inside it, then took from out of her dress a fish head and laid it at the entrance to the cave.

"Let us live," she begged. "Let Helgi have luck with the fishing. Let me live until the money comes and I can go to the harbour. This is all I have to offer. Let me live so I can go to New Iceland. Have mercy."

The wind came then and brought with it rain and sleet. She should have sought refuge in the cave but, instead, she started down, sometimes sliding, sometimes crawling, sometimes tripping and falling, sometimes hanging onto rocks so as not to be blown off the mountain. When she reached the quaking bog, others ran out to lift and carry her. Her body was covered in cuts and bruises. She lay in bed two days and she had to have cloth wrapped around her feet for a week. She didn't remember the trip down.

There were no more landslides and no more sheep went missing. When Helgi returned, his horses were piled high with fish. Sigga saw them, and her mouth filled with saliva.

When she told Helgi she was leaving for Ameríka as soon as her brothers sent her the rest of the money to pay for a ticket, he said, "I might have married you when things improved."

"It's too late," she replied. "I've dreamt of New Iceland."

When the money came, she walked all the way to the coast. Here she stayed until the ship came from England. As it left the harbour, she looked back toward where she thought the farm would be and she thought not of the farm, nor the people there, but of the cave and the one fish head, and the troll, and what it was like alone on the wind- and snow-swept side of the mountain. She bowed her head then and she prayed for those at the farm, she prayed that they would always have enough to eat, that her going would mean more for everyone. She wished things had been different, because Helgi was a good man, and if there were hope for the future, she would have married him. As she held tightly on to the rail of the ship, she prayed for everyone on the farm, she prayed for them because they had no brothers to send them the price of a passage to Ameríka.

INGRID OF THE LAKE

After her farm chores were finished, Ingrid had gone swimming and an unexpected current had pulled her far from shore. Both the sky and the water were turning dark. She could no longer see the shore and only had a faint glimmer of sunlight to the west to guide her.

There were no islands nearby, and the chance of someone in a boat, in the falling dusk, seeing her blonde tresses floating on the surface was unlikely, if not impossible. "Séra Jón," she thought, "where are those miracles of which you preach on Sundays?" She lay on her back, barely moving her hands and feet, too tired to fight the current. She thought of all the young men who had come to court her. Where were they now that she needed them? If one of them were to appear and pull her to safety, she'd promise to marry him.

Her father and mother had warned her of the danger of swimming alone and far from shore. Her mother was a tall, thin woman who sat on a psalm book at parties so as not to be tempted to the devil's work. Her father was shorter and broader and not overly optimistic about the world. If Ingrid said, "It's going to be a fine day today," he replied, "If the weather doesn't change." Her mother had also warned her of the danger of dancing and frivolous clothes and flirting, of letting young men walk her home from church, of looking too long in the mirror.

"I'll be relieved," her father said, as if her beauty were a great burden, "when you're safely married with children."

There was more than enough to do on the farm. Like most small farms, it was set close to the lakeshore so that the farmer could also fish. There was not enough in butter and wool to make a living.

She had heard drowning did not hurt, was even pleasant, but she'd seen the bodies of fishermen washed ashore and they were not smiling. Their faces were blue and grey and blotched, their mouths open, their eyes staring. Swimming was beyond her now. She thought she should have let the current take her, not struggled against it and now that it was weaker, she might have escaped its grasp.

She closed her eyes for a moment, then opened them as she felt the water eddying around her legs. She rolled over onto her front and saw a large, dark shadow moving beneath her. She was frightened. She had heard of monsters in the lake, things that rose out of the darkness. Something surfaced beside her, then sank out of sight, surfaced again, this time closer, and was still. It looked like it might have been a large log.

She grabbed hold of it. It was hard and smooth but it was not a log. There were ridges on it like plates of armour. She rested for a few minutes. When she opened her eyes, in the light of the rising moon, she saw a tail moving slowly in the water.

She knew what she was holding on to because only sturgeon, great beasts from prehistoric times, grew this large in Lake Winnipeg. They were as long as a skiff. When a sturgeon was caught, a man in the bow had to hold the head while a man in the stern held the tail. Fishermen hated them because they left great, gaping holes in their nets. They also hunted them because their eggs and flesh could be sold in the city for a high price.

Since the sturgeon did not move, she pulled herself onto it. She rested there, her body lying along its length; it was longer than she was. She thought she slept because she was sure she dreamt. In her dream she swam without breathing, over the bottom of the lake, in and out of under-ground caves, past the foot of cliffs, into a river where she lay still on the bottom. When she woke she was cold. Startled, she slipped off the sturgeon but managed to grab on to the fish's bony ridge. As she lay beside it, the sturgeon began to swim, and since she had neither the strength nor any idea of what direction to swim in the darkness, she let it pull her along. When she turned her head and looked up, the moon hung there like a golden disc, and the stars were so thick they turned the sky white.

A light appeared. It was small and weak, but gradually it became stronger and then there was a dark line she knew must be the shore. When she bumped against the sandy bottom, she let go of the fish and stumbled to her feet. She staggered forward and then fell to her knees. The sturgeon was lying mostly out of the water. She wept and tears dripped onto its head. Slowly the sturgeon turned and disappeared. She realized she was close to where she had entered the water.

Instead of the windows of her parents' house being dark, they were brightly lit. When she opened the door and stood in the entrance, the room was filled with downcast neighbours comforting her mother and father. When she saw Ingrid, her mother clapped her hands to her face.

"I'm not a ghost," Ingrid said. "I'm alive."

One of the women put out her hand and touched her. "Cold," she said.

"I'll be warm in a little while," Ingrid replied. "The current took me away but I'm a strong swimmer and eventually it released me."

Someone brought her a towel and helped her to get dry. Another wrapped her in a blanket. "Ghosts don't drink coffee," she said as she sipped at her cup.

"Unless they've been raised up," said Garður from Grund. "Then they want their fair share."

The next morning she said nothing about what had happened. She went about her chores milking the cows, feeding the chickens and the sheep. That evening after supper, her mother said, "You aren't going swimming again?"

"It's been a hot day," Ingrid replied. "I need to wash myself clean."

Her parents watched anxiously as she waded into the lake. Although the sun shone from the surface, the water was dark and full of secrets.

Ingrid swam close to the shore that first day, but each day after that, she swam further and further out as if she were looking for something. Now a change came over Ingrid's mother. Those things that her mother had so feared, she encouraged. She asked young men to come over for coffee and cards. She encouraged her husband to clear the loft and hire a fiddler for a dance. She took Ingrid with her to visit every household. She talked of the joy of being a wife and mother. She no longer sat on her psalm book at parties.

"Something enchanted her," she said to her husband. "She is with us but her mind is drifting and when she spins or knits, her eyes are always on the water."

The next time Séra Jón came to give a sermon at the church, Ingrid's mother asked him to visit. That evening, she asked him if her daughter was under a spell. He talked to Ingrid but said he could see nothing different except she seemed more serious but that was not surprising. Those who have confronted death often think more deeply than they did before. He prayed over her and she prayed with him. It made no difference. When she woke in the morning, the first thing she did was look out over the lake. The last thing she did at night was study the water.

She swam, not just on the surface, but below the surface, diving deep, staying down until someone watching would have thought she might have drowned. Visitors seeing her commented on it. "Like a fish," they said to her parents. "If she's in the water much more, she'll develop gills."

"What is it she searches for in the darkness of the lake?" others asked. They were superstitious and the depths, for them, held unimaginable terrors. When her mother brushed Ingrid's hair, she watched her neck for any sign of scales. Some said she had learned to breathe underwater. Others said that she'd been enchanted.

Finally, her father forbade her swimming. "There's too much gossip," he said.

Although she obeyed him, her thoughtfulness turned to melancholy.

She went to the shore but not into the water. She carded wool more than ever. She spun and knitted long into the night. Some said she used wake-picks to keep her eyes open. She grew thin and her health began to fail.

Her father's nets, even when other men's nets were empty, had always been full. Now, his nets held nothing but sticks and weeds. Great holes appeared in some of them. Other nets disappeared, pulled away by the current and, if he managed to find them by dragging, they came up a tangled, torn mess. On a calm night, his skiff broke loose from its mooring and drifted onto the rocks.

Ingrid's mother called on Séra Jón again. This time when he came, Ingrid told him the story of the sturgeon.

"Is it not something like Jonah and the whale?" she asked. "I have heard people tell of shipwrecked fishermen in Iceland being pushed to shore by whales and seals."

Séra Jón admitted he'd heard such stories, had even met one man to whom it had happened. Still, he performed an exorcism.

Afterwards, Ingrid's father gave her permission to go swimming again. To stop the gossip she no longer swam during the day but only after the sun had set. Her health came back. Once, her father saw her returning just after dawn.

In the fall as the ice was beginning to form, one of the farmers rode up to see Ingrid's father. A great sturgeon had been sighted in the creek to the north. The farmer was gathering men to build a fence across the creek. The sturgeon's flesh would help pay for their winter's supplies. They gathered together, a dozen or more men to cut willow. They sharpened the ends, drove the stems into the mud, and then interwove the willow to make a screen across the mouth. Children ran along the bank, throwing stones into the water, kneeling over the edge to see if the sturgeon might be lying in the undercut.

Ingrid went down to watch but stood some distance away with her arms crossed over her chest. The fence was not completed until the evening. The farmers all went home to sharpen their knives and axes on their whetstones. That evening when she went out there was already frost in the air. The last her father saw of her, she was walking on the beach.

In the morning the willow screen had been destroyed. Pieces were floating on the surface and tossed up on the bank. Some said during the night the sturgeon had used its great strength to thrash against the fence, ripping it apart. Others, when they heard Ingrid was not to be found, said she had slipped into the water and, riding on the sturgeon's back, had pulled the fence apart, then went with him into the lake.

Although for many nights her father went to the shore and hung a lantern on a pole, Ingrid did not return. Some said that, having been saved by the kindness of the sturgeon, Ingrid could not bear the cruelty of men and had gone away to live by herself on an island. Ármann from Arnafjörður said she'd been bewitched by a *hafmaður*. He may have been right about her being bewitched because, over the passing years, fishermen reported two sturgeon sunning themselves in the shallows. Hunting them proved fruitless. It was believed they lived most of the time in the underground lake that joins Lake Winnipeg to Lake Manitoba.

Her mother and father tried to ignore the gossip about her disappearance. If anyone brought it up, they said she must have gone swimming and been caught in the current.

Her father searched the shoreline for many weeks. When he did not find his daughter's body, he stopped fishing. He was afraid he might find evidence of his daughter in his nets. Her mother found comfort in her Bible and often said, "The Lord works in mysterious ways." Finally, because of the rumours, they paid for a full funeral service at Riverton. They buried an empty coffin. That, they said, was the end of it, but people noticed that when the lake was free of ice, her parents always set a lamp in the window.

LOFTUR

When Sigurbjörg knelt over the stream on her father's farm, she saw a young woman with long blond hair that waved and curled at the ends, a young woman with fine features and pale blue eyes. When men saw her, they wanted her for a wife. They came to court her, bringing small gifts to give her mother and father to enlist them in their suit. Sigurbjörg turned them all down.

"Too fussy," her mother complained. "Thorður has a good home field. Ragnar has cows. Bergir has a fine boat. If you would marry, there'd be more room and food for the rest of us."

"Thorður," Sigurbjörg replied, "is older than my father. Ragnar is a drunkard and everyone knows Bergir used to beat his wife."

"Páll! You want to marry Páll!" her mother exclaimed. "His home field is small, he only has a few cows and sheep, he has no boat."

"He's only five years older than me. He doesn't spend his money on brandy. He wouldn't beat his wife," Sigurbjörg said. "Besides, he owns enough land to be able to marry."

It would have been easier for the vanity of the other suitors if Páll had been wealthy, or large, or strong. He was not. He was average height, slightly built and inclined to be a dreamer. Sigurbjörg's mother said he thought too much about poetry and not enough about lambs. Poetry would never help feed them.

"That's fine," Sigurbjörg said, "I know how to work."

"It's as easy to love a man with a lot of sheep as a man with few sheep," her mother muttered, but she did not protest too loudly, for with Sigurbjörg gone, there was one less mouth to feed. The *skyr* and the smoked mutton would last longer.

It should have ended there. Sigurbjörg should have had children, organized their farm, kept Páll focused enough on their sheep and cows and haymaking to feed and clothe them. But her suitors, rejected for someone they thought not as strong, not as well off, not as important, were not just jealous but insulted and, sharing their anger, decided on revenge for what they saw as a slight on their manhood. They hired a man, Snorri, who lived alone on the edge of the Sprengisandur desert. It was said he kept a rune in one shoe and a piece of human skull in the other to make his spells more powerful.

They paid him well with dried fish and butter so he would call up a ghost to torment Páll and Sigurbjörg. They chose the ghost of an outlaw who had starved to death during the Móðuharðindin, the great death mist, around a hundred years before, and whose spirit, it was said, still roamed the mountain trails looking for food.

When the Laki volcano erupted, Jón Steingrímsson, the Lutheran minister, gave a sermon that caused a river of lava to divide and flow around his church. It saved his parishoners, who had sought refuge there, but it didn't save Loftur or ten thousand others. It didn't save the eighty percent of the cattle who died from the fluorine and sulphur dioxide that spread like fog.

This ghost was said to have broken into a larder at Reykjahlíð by Mývatn and stolen dried fish heads. Rumour had it he'd driven a sheep over a cliff since he had no other way of killing it. When it was found, it had been half-eaten.

This was the ghost of the man called Loftur. When Loftur was young, he'd taken a small holding at the very edge of the mountains. In good years, there was grass, enough, at least, that he could feed his cattle and sheep. In bad years all his bones showed. The farmers claimed he lived by stealing their sheep because they could see no other way he could get enough to eat. The land was rugged, with many cliffs and cold rushing rivers, and sheep went missing with not even their bones being found. It might have been the fate of sheep to get lost and die in sudden snow storms or fall into a *gjá* but at the annual *rétt*, when not as many sheep were rounded up as expected, the talk always turned to Loftur.

Once, when the farmers were determined to prove he was the cause of their misfortune, a group of them rode up to his hut, which was nothing more than a small mound made of stone and turf; because, how much space does a man by himself need? It was, the farmers said, like living in a grave, and they wondered if he was not already a dead man and if they were not seeing his ghost. They muttered to themselves when they found no sheep's heads with the ears cut off to hide their ownership, no bones at the edge of the bog but, finally, they mounted their horses and left.

When the death mist came, the grass didn't grow and Loftur's animals did not survive. He took to the mountain tracks but no farm wanted him. Instead of offering him milk, they told him to drink from the river and dine on the sheep that he'd already stolen. Desperate, he did steal fish from the drying sheds, he did butcher a lamb, and he lived in caves and in shelters made from stone. His clothes turned to rags and when, finally, someone found his remains at the side of a path, they thought at first it was just a pile of worthless cloth. His only possession was a copy of the *Passíusálmar*. His body and the *Passion Hymns* were buried under a pile of stones.

Loftur's ghost was sent to Páll and Sigurbjörg's farm. He was instruct-ed to haunt and harass the family for three generations.

For a time, Loftur did nothing; but then he started to get up to mis-chief. He chased the sheep so one of them lost a lamb. He called the ravens to the farm so they croaked all night and no one could sleep. One night there was a high wind and even though everyone was inside, they heard a voice calling, *come with me, come with me*, but no one dared go outside for fear the ghost would lead them to the cliffs. Once, when the milk was left unattended, Loftur put a lump of dirt in it. When the hired hands were working outside, he caused a great wind that suddenly pelted them with sticks and stones. None of his tricks were life-threatening but they left everyone unsettled. The sheep and cows were as tormented as if they had been in a cloud of midges and they produced less and less milk. The horses were skittish and grew thin. There had been no foxes here for years but Loftur brought two foxes that worried the sheep.

Páll and Sigurbjörg talked about going to the magician and paying him to lift the spell, but they knew it was no use. Whatever they could afford to pay, the rejected suitors could afford to pay more.

To make matters worse, some of the rejected suitors began to make threats and claim that Páll had taken some of their land and they were going to start lawsuits to take it back. Sigurbjörg grew thin with worry. Páll, seeing this, wrote less and less poetry, and worked harder at the farming but, at every turn, his efforts were thwarted. He tried to drain his land but the ditches became plugged again. He cut turf for burning but the piles were tossed about.

As they lay in bed one evening, Sigurbjörg said, "I dreamt of going on a voyage. I was on a ship."

Páll was a great believer in dreams. He told her to think about this dream as she was going to sleep. She did and in the morning, she said that she had dreamt of many people, strangers, and a place where the birch trees grew to the sky.

"Ameríka," Pál said. "The *bændur* say it's a land of savages and wilderness. Everyone who goes there will die. They have been trying to keep the immigration agents from visiting the farms." He was not surprised she had dreamt of a distant land because, in spite of the *bændur*, the large land owners, trying to keep people from learning about Ameríka, meetings were held. Recently, there had been a meeting at a nearby farm. Letters from Ameríka had arrived and those had been read, and then passed on from farm to farm. Some letters had been published in newspapers.

Rumours had been spread about how the Indians would attack the settlers, but letters published in the newspaper said the Indians had shown the Icelanders nothing but kindness.

"Many may die on the way to the New World, but many who stay here will die," Sigurbjörg said. "Besides, I don't want to bear any man's child except yours."

They were silent then because Páll knew what she meant. The women who were kept as paupers at some farms had no choice but to have sex with the farmer. It was the farmer who decided if she had shelter or food. Many times such women became pregnant. The farmer's wife always blamed the pauper and so she was put up for bids again. Such women were moved from farm to farm. Sigurbjörg's jealous suitors had more than one way of getting what they wanted.

"We should go while we still have something to sell," Sigurbjörg added.

Lying on his back, staring into the darkness, thinking of his land and cattle, of his home field and the mountains beyond, Páll finally said, "A ghost and lawsuits cannot travel across the ocean."

He was right about the farmers' lawsuits but wrong about the ghost. He and Sigurbjörg left for Ameríka and settled in a cabin on the shore of Lake Winnipeg. The cabin had been abandoned by earlier settlers who had moved on to Dakota Territory. Sigurbjörg was large with child and was unable to help Páll clear land. They had a shed for a cow and three sheep and a haystack large enough to feed their animals during the winter months.

"Did you talk to the man on the beach?" she asked Páll one day. He shook his head. "I saw him when I was collecting driftwood for the fire. He was wearing ragged clothes."

Just after that their cow became so frightened it ran away. To survive the coming winter they had to have milk. Their child would need it. From the milk they made *skyr* and cheese and butter. They kept the whey for drinking. In spite of being plagued by mosquitoes and flies, Páll searched the swamps. He managed to find the cow standing in an open area where there were not so many mosquitoes and flies.

"The ragged man has followed us far," Páll said. Now that they were going to have a child, he worried, because mischief with a child could be fatal. "I'll see if I can find a minister who will lay him to rest."

He went to a neighbour's and the neighbour asked another and soon the word had spread that someone was needed to return a ghost to the soil, but there was no one who had come who knew the rune poems, who harboured the secrets of the Black School. One woman came but she only chanted some verses from the Bible and she might as well have been a wind from the lake; except the wind, at least, made the grass bend before it.

Páll had managed to build a small, flat-bottomed boat and Sigurbjörg sewed him a net that he could set just offshore. He caught fish that they ate fresh. He smoked some fish, and when Sigurbjörg cleaned and split pickerel to the tail and removed the backbone, he hung the fish above the fly line so they would dry for the winter.

Once, after Páll had set his nets, Loftur stirred them around, but he was no wiser than any others living in this new place and his old tricks were not so effective in Ameríka.

Páll saw Loftur one day on the beach. Páll was afraid for them, for the unborn child, and being afraid, anger rose in him. He chased Loftur down the beach, grabbed him and tried to throw him down, but the angrier he became, the stronger Loftur became and, finally, Loftur lifted him up and threw him into the shallow water along the beach. Then he disappeared.

The next evening as Páll was carding wool and Sigurbjörg was knitting mittens, she said, "I feel sorry for Loftur."

"Why?" Páll replied. "He plagues us."

"Think of his life. There was no Ameríka for him. It is hard here but we have our own land. Things will get better. We are not taxed by the church. Some have more than others but there are no farmers here who have all the power."

Páll was silent. Although he'd owned a small-holding and had been better off than many, he'd felt the injustice of the farmers who were wealthy and powerful.

"He carried the *Passíusálmar*," Sigurbjörg added. "If he was such a bad person, why was it with him when he died? I often think of that."

They both knew Loftur's story. They thought of how easy it would have been, with the way the law was, the harshness of the weather, the vindictiveness of the farmers, for them to lose what they had and become paupers. Here, they cleared their own ground. They collected their own wood. Páll fished just off shore without hindrance.

"I will write a poem for him," Páll said. He wrote about hunger and cold and despair. He read it aloud to Sigurbjörg, and she said, because she was able to imagine herself on a wind- and rain-swept trail in the mountains without food or shelter, "What would Loftur want most but something to eat and a place to stay?"

The next morning, Sigurbjörg set out a piece of butter on a third plate. She put it in the shed with the cow. When she went back, it was gone.

"He was turned away," Páll said. "If it were me, I'd hate those who turned me away to die on a mountain path in the cold and rain."

Their place was small but they made a pallet and Páll wrote another poem, welcoming Loftur, telling him here was a place for him. He did not need to sleep in the cold. What they had, they would share. He read it aloud that evening.

The food Sigurbjörg put out always disappeared and, gradually, the feeling that someone was with them changed from a feeling of anger and revenge to one of contentment and help. Their cow no longer ran away. The nets stayed where they were set. When their daughter was born, they felt as though someone looked over her. When Páll cleared land and cut wood, he felt, sometimes, as if someone was helping him, because he did things he did not think possible.He lifted logs and rocks, rowed his boat against the current, dragged his cow from a mud hole. It was as if someone worked with him.

In the evening, as they worked, they always had a third stool for Loftur so he could sit with them and they talked about how good it was to sit there, warm from the stove, instead of struggling over mountain trails, unfed.

They set a third plate at the table. What they set out was always gone in the morning.

Páll wrote a poem and Sigurbjörg read it aloud, promising Loftur they would never turn anyone away who came to their door in need and they would teach their children and grandchildren to do the same. They prospered and built a frame house. In only one way was it different from most houses. It had in it a small room with a cot on which no one was allowed to sleep. There were warm blankets and always a bit of food on a plate. It was Loftur's room.

Their daughter, Fjóla, was allowed to visit the room, to sit on the bed, to put flowers in a glass jar, but it was not her room. It was Loftur's room and when some people said they should just use it for storage, they always smiled and shook their heads, because they understood from sitting in the evenings with Loftur, what it was like to be without food, without a place to stay, to struggle through wind and rain and snow, to have rags for clothes and to have no hope—and then to have a place of one's own.

THE POET FROM ARNES

Snjolaug's husband, Oskar, drowned during a sudden blow from the northeast. Winds come up so suddenly on Lake Winnipeg that even the most experienced of fishermen are caught by surprise. It was late in the season and Oskar had been pulling up his nets. The local fishermen thought his skiff must have plunged to the bottom before Oskar could dump the anchors that would have been hooked over the gunwales. His skiff, low in the water, would have easily been swamped. Even so, they expected to find some debris such as fish box lids or oars.

"Nothing," they said to each other, their thoughts turned inward by the oddness of it.

It was odder still when, after three days, he didn't float. He could, however, have become entangled in rope or nets. They all wore oil skins, heavy waterproof pants and jackets, which might have held a man down.

The local fishermen pulled up Oskar's nets and delivered them to his widow. They were relieved he wasn't in them. They hated it when anyone drowned because none of them wanted to lift a net heavy with fish only to find it was not fish but one of their neighbours tangled in the mesh. Still, they kept an eye open in case he floated but Oskar did not float. They searched the shore where the current eddied and swirled but there was nothing there except driftwood and clumps of reeds and muddy rocks.

Good men are hard to find and Oskar was one of the best. He was gentle with his cows, dipping his hands in warm water before beginning milking. His door was open to anyone passing by. He could scythe hay from dawn to dusk. If he had a fault, it was his spending too much time singing. Not that it was a fault exactly but, sometimes, when he should have been cleaning out the barn or fixing a fence, he was writing music or off singing at some event. He had a fine voice and was a regular in the church choir.

Snjolaug had not married him because of his voice. She'd married him because he had a dozen cows and a two-story, narrow clapboard house. It had two bedrooms upstairs with an iron bedstead in each, a kitchen, a parlour downstairs, and a root cellar she could enter through a trap door in the kitchen floor. Although Snjolaug owned only one recipe book, and that was the one published by the Lutheran Ladies' Aid, she was a good cook. The recipes leaned heavily to fish or meat with mashed potatoes.

The cows were unsettled by Oskar's disappearance. They were used to Oskar singing to them as he worked in the barn. Snjolaug was much more businesslike. She was not unkind, but rather efficient and silent. If she had sung anything, it would have been a hymn and, if she had recited anything, it would have been the Lord's Prayer. Where the cows had given milk with love, they now gave milk with obedience. There was little real difference except for a bit less butterfat.

Snjolaug wasn't sure what to do. If Oskar's body had floated after three days as it should have, everything would be settled. She wasn't sure if she should clear out the second bedroom that he used for a study—give his belongings to the church for needy parishioners, and his books to the local library kept in Gunnar Finnson's front parlour—or whether she should leave everything just as it was. The problem was solved when a schoolteacher turned up on her doorstep, suitcase in hand, saying she had heard there was an extra room at Snjolaug's.

She hesitated for a moment, but with only the dairy cows and sheep bringing in an income, she was a bit short. She wrapped Oskar's clothes in brown paper and packed them into two clean fish boxes. She sorted through his books. The only practical books were a book about caring for cattle and another on sheep. She wished he'd spent more time reading these. She kept those out. Songbooks with his handwritten notes filled most of the shelves. Although she resented the time he spent singing instead of farming, she had to admit he had the voice of an angel. When he sang "*Góða Nótt*" at the end of a funeral, there wasn't a dry eye anywhere in the church.

She had been—and still was—a good wife. People said you could eat off her floors. She cleaned them on her knees. She had a fine hand when she sewed. She made all her own clothes. Hats she bought at the general store. She schooled herself not to make careless statements for they quickly turned into lies. Vanity and self-importance did that. She made the desserts Oskar liked—*mysuostur* and *sætsúpa*—because he had a sweet tooth, but she did not make them too often. Gluttony, after all, was a sin. She refused to make *ástarbollur*. The name, love balls, embarrassed her. She made *kleinur* instead.

Over their bed hung a picture of them on their wedding day. They were no longer young when they married, so they weren't at their best. She was sitting and he was standing. She'd insisted on that because she was a bit taller than him. There were pictures of their seven nieces and nephews. There was, she thought with a touch of sorrow and bitterness, no picture of a child of their own.

She finished packing his music. It filled three boxes. He was always singing. He never missed a practice. Many times, when the road was blocked with snowdrifts, he went on snowshoes. The choir sang on Sundays, but it also sang at special events. Oskar was often asked to sing at funerals and weddings. Although he was seldom given more than a free meal, he never turned down an invitation.

She was grateful for the cows. Without them, he'd have been gadding about, singing here and there. The cows needed milking every day. That kept him from being like other men she knew, appearing and disappearing. She hadn't wanted to marry any of the whitefishermen for that reason. They were always going north to the fishing grounds instead of fishing from home. She'd wanted a man she could keep an eye on. Of course, she'd expected by now that they'd have had family to take care of. They'd even talked about how Oskar would build an addition onto the house when children came.

Her boarder was a nice young woman. A bit flighty for someone with so much responsibility but she wasn't a fussy eater, she didn't snore and she remembered to take off her shoes when she came into the house.

The teacher had been boarding with her for seven months when Oskar returned. He was wearing the same clothes as when he had disappeared.

Other women might have fainted or screamed, but Snjolaug, after a quick jerk of the head when she saw Oskar's overalls and Oskar in them out in the yard, started breakfast. He milked the cows before he came in. She looked out the parlour window and saw his boat pulled onto the shore. When he did come inside, he sat in his usual place, eating his bacon and eggs and toast as if he'd never been away. She made him an extra two pieces of toast. She could see he hadn't been eating well. He was quite a bit thinner than when he'd disappeared and he had a nervous tic over his right eye. If there were any real change, it was that he seemed more distracted than usual, the way he was when he was writing songs.

Fifteen minutes after she realized who Oskar was, the teacher was scurrying down the road, suitcase in hand.

She spread the word of Oskar's return throughout the area. People turned up to see for themselves. The women sat nervously in the kitchen, perched on the edges of their chairs, wanting to ask questions but not quite daring to come out and inquire about where he had been. It wouldn't have done them any good. Oskar behaved as if he'd never been away. Their husbands went over to where Oskar was fixing a fence and cleared their throats a lot and shared some snuff but they, too, left with their questions unasked.

"If it's really Oskar," people whispered, "he'll come to church and sing in the choir. If it's not, he'll not come within the hearing of the church bell."

Oskar came to church and though the sexton rang the bell long and loud, Oskar never turned a hair. However, he did not sing. He did not sing at the farm, either. When he was invited to sing at special events, he just smiled and gave a quick shake of his head. After a while, people quit asking him. Snjolaug wished, now, that he would sing. She sometimes stopped outside the barn to hear if he sang quietly to the cows. There was silence.

"Why don't you sing?" she asked one day. "The choir needs you. If you won't sing for them, sing for me."

He smiled and shook his head.

One fall morning when Snjolaug opened the kitchen door there was a large willow basket on the stoop. She bent down. Wrapped in a blanket there was a child. She stood up and looked about the yard. There was no one in sight. She looked around both sides, of the house, then came back. She picked up the basket, took it inside and put it on the table.

"A child," she said to Oskar. "From nowhere. Just like that." She'd have said more but the child had wakened and started to cry. She picked him up, then sent Oskar for warm milk from a cow. When she unwrapped the child, she saw he had dark eyes and hair and skin, while she and Oskar were blue-eyed, blond-haired and fair-skinned; but there was something familiar about him.

A child isn't a secret. Those who had come to see Oskar after his return now came to peer at the child. Snjolaug had replaced his moss diaper with cloth and made him cotton nightgowns. She began to knit baby clothes. The first while after the child appeared, Snjolaug listened for a footstep or a knock at the door. If she could have, she would have hardened her heart against the child for fear of what it would feel like when his mother came to claim him.

No one came and the child snared her heart with his smile. Snjolaug made him a stuffed lamb and covered it with wool from one of their sheep.

Oskar made a bassinette. He ordered a rocking chair. Fall soon turned to winter. They put up a Christmas tree and laid presents under it.

Snjolaug watched the road and when someone knocked at the door, her heart leapt with fear. When no one had come by the following spring, she said, "We'll foster him." It was common among the Icelandic families to foster children. Those who had too many often shared with those who had none. This was not the first child to be left on someone's steps.

One day, when she was humming a lullaby because the child was crying, she said to Oskar, "Sing to him. I can't keep a tune. If you sang to him, it would soothe him."

Oskar just shook his head.

No one came that summer, or the next, or the summer after that. Kjartan—that was what they named him—loved to run in the field and pick flowers, so they planted a flower garden together that he might pick flowers to his heart's content.

Oskar and Snjolaug's lives changed in ways impossible to describe. Where there had been silence, there was laughter; where averted eyes, they looked at each other and smiled; where they read alone in the evening, they sat with Kjartan and read aloud to him in English and Icelandic. They made plans. Snjolaug said things like "You'll have to teach him to skate," and Oskar replied she'd need to show him how to write his Icelandic letters. If their neighbours had been asked about any change they'd noticed, they'd have said, "They're happy."

All this time, Oskar said nothing about the time he had been gone. There were rumours, of course. That he'd run away with Juliana, the young woman who'd been in the choir but had moved to the city. That he'd had a blow to his head and had amnesia until one day he recovered his memory and found himself living in some distant village. The truth was stranger than that.

The storm on the day he disappeared had come late in the season. There was already ice along the shore. He'd been caught pulling the last of his nets out of the water. The wind nearly blew him out of the boat. Waves rose to over eight feet. When he rode them up, he thought the skiff might tip backward and when he rode over the crest into the trough, the skiff stood nearly vertical. The wind was bitter cold and the spray, when it struck both him and the boat, turned to ice. Soon the boat wallowed with the extra weight. He had all he could do to keep the skiff from turning sideways in the troughs. Soon, ice formed a thick lump in his moustache and beard.

The storm lasted all night. His skiff was foundering when the waves drove him onto a beach. He climbed over the gunwale and fell into the surf. Somehow, he managed to drag the skiff high enough that the waves could not pull it back. He dropped onto his knees and rested his head against the boat. He knew then he would die. The ice was like an iron mask. He banged his face against the gunwale to try to break the ice free.

That is when a woman appeared. She was wrapped in a deerskin and he could not see her face. She did not speak and he could not. She helped him to his feet and then led him to shelter. He remembered nothing of the next few days but broken images and when he was himself again, the world was locked in ice. He stayed with her all that winter. All that winter he sang to her. He sang every song he knew. He wrote songs on birch bark with a charcoal stick and sang those. When the ice broke up and leaves began to appear, he repaired his boat.

"What do you want most?" she asked as she stood in the knee-deep water, holding the gunwale. "I'll give you anything you want."

"What I can't have," he said. "A son."

As he fitted the oars to the oarlocks, she rested her hand on his arm. "I'll give you that," she said, taking his hand and pressing it to her heart, "but promise me that you'll never sing for anyone else."

He kept his promise until his son's wedding day. It was then Snjolaug insisted he sing. "Can you not sing for your son?" she asked. "How can you say you love him? One song. What harm would it do? You love him, but don't love him enough for that."

So, he sang. One of his songs about love and the warmth of a fire in the darkness, of shadows and light, of passion, of love won and lost.

That night Kjartan vanished. It was as if he'd never been. He and his bride were staying in a cabin by the lake and it was thought, at first, that he might have gone swimming and drowned. However, none of his clothes were found. He didn't float. He stepped into the darkness and disappeared.

Oskar and Snjolaug lived for a long time after that but things were never the way they had been. Where she had, at one time, feared the sound of a footfall on the steps or a knock on the door, now she hoped for them. Oskar did not sing again. However, he continued to write songs in English and Icelandic, and collections of his music can still be seen on bookshelves here and there in New Iceland.

HALLDÓR VITLAUS

At first they called him Halldór Fiskur. That was before he shot the wolf. After a while they called him Halldór Vitlaus. Halldór the Witless. His fish camp was at Humbug Bay.

There was no benefit in shooting the wolf. It is true that it howled at the full moon and it came to the shore to drink from the lake. However, its howling kept no one awake and there would have to have been a thousand thousand wolves to drink the lake dry. He also shot the wolf in July, when its pelt was of no value.

It happened this way. Halldór had noticed the wolf tracks in the sand. Curious, he'd started to watch at dawn and dusk. The wolves were like shadows for though he kept finding tracks in the sand, he did not manage to see the wolves for many days. Finally, one morning, just as the sun was making the eastern horizon pink, he saw them slip out of the dark forest. There were six of them. A couple he'd seen on the ice for more than one winter and four pups. The male was big, black. The female was white and smaller. The pups were two brown, one white and one black. The adults sniffed the air and turned their heads this way and that. They all waited for the black one to go to the water. Only when he began to drink did the others follow.

Halldór watched them for six mornings. He could not have told you why, but one morning he took his rifle with him and sat with it across his knees. He crouched in the shadows under the dock. The pups were chasing each other, playfighting, rolling in the sand. He shot the black leader. When the bullet struck him, he leapt into the air with a startled bark, then dropped to the sand. The others whirled away. Halldór shot again but the bullet only hit a tree. He waited under the dock a while to see if the wolf would move, or if the other wolves, out of curiosity, would come back.

When neither happened, he crept out of the darkness. He pushed the body with his toe. He skinned the wolf and stretched the skin on a frame. He took it to a woman who knew how to tan hides. She tanned it and sewed red felt to the back so he could use it for a carpet.

Other fishermen heard what he had done. When they stopped by the camp they said, "What'd you do that for?" They all shot a moose in the fall. Or, if a bear started raiding their camp, terrifying the cook or stealing meat from the ice house, they'd track it down. They killed nothing without a reason and, unless you wanted wolf fur to trim parkas, there was no reason to shoot them. Halldór just shrugged. He would have told them why if he had known, but he didn't know.

After that when he went into the bush to cut tamarack poles, he felt as if he were being watched. He would pause and listen. He started to take his rifle with him. He kept it within reach. Sometimes, the bush would rustle and he'd pick up the rifle and fire a shot at the sound. Eventually, he quit going into the bush unless someone were with him.

"I shoulda shot them all," he said to a fisherman who'd stopped by to visit.

In the off-seasons he lived alone. He never meant to be an old bachelor with nothing but a radio for company. He only went to town when he needed supplies. During the fishing season he kept three men on shares. He provided the equipment, charged the men board and room, and kept a percentage of their fish.

"You're bushed," said Gunnar, one of the fishermen, after Halldór told him about being watched.

"The devil has many helpers," Halldór said. "Look at their eyes. They'd rip your throat out for no reason."

When the leaves fell from the trees, Halldór was relieved. It made it easier to see anything lurking in the bush. He cut back the bush so there was more open space. When he was caulking the boats, he kept his rifle propped against a fish box.

"A wolf," he said, pushing at the carpet with his boot. "What's a wolf? They kill cattle."

There were no cattle there, of course. Only fishermen and the one-eyed cook who always burned the bacon. Winter came. They put on snowshoes to go out on first ice. That is the best time for catching pickerel. They brought the best prices. It was dangerous, though. The ice was like rubber, stretching, sinking beneath them. When they cut holes, the water welled up and flooded the ice.

The weather grew colder, the ice hardened, grew rough. Snow drifted across it. They set gangs of nets far out onto the lake. They pulled their sled with a piebald horse. They'd been fishing for a week when the wolves started following them from hole to hole. The wolves, that in past years had come close, now stayed well away, behind the broken ice that had been forced up into mounds.

"They're hunting me," Halldór said.

"They want the scrap fish we leave at the holes," Gunnar replied. "It's an easy meal."

Halldór took his rifle with him after that. Sometimes he'd fire a shot at the wolves but with the drifting snow and glare of the ice, hitting anything was unlikely. As soon as he fired, the wolves would scatter, running back toward the shore. In a little while, though, they'd return.

"I told you," Halldór said. "That white one. I recognize her."

"I haven't seen many moose tracks this winter," Ragnar, one of the hired men, said. "Not many rabbits. If you don't want them following us, don't leave maria at the holes."

That gave Halldór an idea. He took five maria back to the camp, slit their bellies, put in some old fish hooks, then set the fish outside to freeze.

The next day he dropped the maria off at the first hole. When the fishermen returned, the fish were still there.

The hired men saw the fish and looked at each other but said nothing.

Every shadow became a wolf. At every sound Halldór would go to the door, rifle in hand. One night Gunnar was returning from the outhouse when he saw Halldór aiming the rifle at him. "What are you doing?" he asked. I've been fishing for you for ten years. Maybe longer. Why are you pointing a rifle at me?"

"I thought you…" Halldór began, looking around. He went inside.

The wolves howled every night. One would begin, then another, then another, until it seemed the camp was surrounded by wolves. "Shut up, shut up," Halldór shouted. He took his rifle to the door and shot into the darkness. There was silence. He went inside. There was a yip, yip, then it was taken up, as if the wolves were talking. Then one broke into a howl. The others followed.

"A full moon," Gunnar said the next morning. "They always howl at a full moon."

Ragnar said he wasn't well. He wanted his pay to take to his wife when he went to see the doctor.

"He won't be back," Halldór said. "He wouldn't look me in the eye."

The next week there was a message from Stephen's wife asking him to come home. Their son was ill. Halldór grimaced. "Ragnar's wife's been talking. Maybe," he said to Gunnar, "you'd like to quit, too."

"I'll stay a while," Gunnar said. "My wife's not expecting me until Christmas."

"It's the wolves," Halldór said. "They're making everyone nervous."

"Not as nervous as you make me," Gunnar said.

They had to pull up some of the nets. There are only so many that two men can lift. The weather had been clear with light winds but now it began to snow regularly. Between the wind and the snow, they could not see more than twenty feet. They'd be working at a hole, pulling up the nets, taking the fish out of the mesh, throwing them into boxes, and the wolves would suddenly appear and disappear. Halldór didn't even have time to reach for his rifle.

"I should have shot the white one," he said bitterly. "The black one would be easier to see."

He was carrying a box of fish to the sleigh when he saw a wolf standing in his path. He yelled and dropped the box. The wolf dashed away.

It snowed the next day and the next. Halldór sat at the table playing solitaire. When it was still snowing on the third day, Gunnar said, "We can't leave the fish in the nets. We've got to lift."

"I dream of them," Halldór said. "I'm running and they're following me. Everywhere I go they're waiting. I dream they're beside my bed."

"They're just wolves," Gunnar replied. "They've always been around. We just never paid attention to them before. They've always followed us from hole to hole. Don't you remember, there was that bold one? He'd crawl towards us on his belly and lie there maybe fifteen feet away. We used to throw the fish at him."

The snow was so thick they couldn't see the ice house.

"I don't want to go out until it's stopped snowing," Halldór said. They went anyway. They had no choice. The nets had to be lifted. There was a steady wind so the snow cut across them as they rode out on the sleigh. They might have been lost in space. There was snow underneath them, snow around them, snow and white clouds above them. At the beginning of the season, they'd stuck small shrubs and branches in the snow to guide them to the nets and back. The snow smothered all sound. Wolves could have walked beside them and not be seen or heard.

At the first hole, they had to shovel the snow clear, then scoop out the ice that had formed. The nets froze into delicate, insubstantial lace. They bent their heads against the wind. The snow still found its way into their hoods. The horse and sleigh were a dim blur.

Suddenly, not three feet away, there was the white wolf. Or Halldór thought it was the white wolf. Only its black nose and yellow eyes had any form. Surprised, she leapt away but so quickly that he was not sure she'd been there at all.

"What is it?" Gunnar asked.

"Nothing," Halldór replied. He wasn't sure if he were awake or dreaming. In his dreams this is how it was.

Later, as they ate their supper, he said, "When you do something wrong, it follows you around. I've noticed that. You drink your paycheque instead of taking it home, it doesn't go away. It keeps following you. You hit a child when you're drunk. You cheat someone on his wages. You lie to your wife."

"You haven't been married in a long time," Gunnar replied.

"No," Halldór said. "Not for a long time."

The lake had frozen early that year. They'd started fishing in mid-November. They all needed a break. Gunnar and the cook were getting a ride to town with the freighter.

Christmas was always a difficult time. Halldór never put up decorations, didn't cut a small tree to put in the cook shack. Instead, he shut off the radio so he wouldn't have to listen to the carols and spent his time mending nets, keeping busy. It was easier when he didn't have any reminders of Christmas.

Gunnar was going to have Christmas with his family but he promised to come back in a week. Gunnar said, "Maybe you should come to town. Have Christmas with us this year?"

Halldór thought about that. Gunnar and his wife had three children and a small house with two bedrooms. The boys slept in one bed. He would have to stay at the hotel. There were rooms above the beer parlour. He could sit in his room by himself or go to the beer parlour. If he went to the beer parlour, he'd drink until he ran out of money. He wouldn't mean to. He never meant to. He only ever meant to have a glass or two while he talked to the other fishermen.

That's why he stayed at the camp. That's why he wouldn't let any of his hired men bring liquor with them when they came to work for him.

There was his wife. She hadn't remarried but he wasn't welcome there anymore. Too many broken lamps. Too many broken promises. Too much yelling. There was his daughter, but she and her husband went to the city at Christmas to stay with his parents. When he did stop to visit, his daughter stood blocking the doorway, clenching and unclenching her hands until she was sure he wasn't drinking. He sometimes thought about his life, tracking it like he'd track a moose. He'd follow the tracks, trying to see how he'd ended up here, living by himself in the bush. Why did the moose turn left instead of right? Why did it bed down here? There were no answers. It did turn left. It did bed down here.

Christmas had been difficult when he was a child. There seldom were gifts, but his mother had made a meal they all liked. Macaroni with extra cheese with wieners on top. Because every child was given a small paper bag of candy and an orange at the Lutheran church, his mother always took them to the Christmas service. Sometimes, they were given two bags.

Christmas was worse after he'd taken some money from his father's dresser drawer to buy a gift for his mother. He hadn't meant to steal it. Earlier in the day, he'd been with his mother when she'd looked in the store window at a pair of brown gloves. Her hands had been red with cold. To keep them warm, she usually pulled her hands up into the sleeves of her parka.

"Think before you do things," his father had shouted. "That money is to buy groceries." His father had marched him down to the store and made him return the gloves. His father pocketed the money and went to the beer parlour.

That was the Christmas before his father left to work up north and never came back. That was three years before his mother had said she was taking the bus to Winnipeg to see the doctor. That evening, he and his brother and sister had waited at the bus stop but she never returned. Someone said she'd kept going all the way to Calgary.

When he'd first moved to the fish camp, he'd gone to town to celebrate the various holidays. It was always the same, beer, lots of loud talking, sometimes fighting. He bought beer for everyone. Sometimes, cigarettes. He had a lot of friends, at least until his money ran out. Once he wasn't buying, they disappeared. After a while, he felt they were laughing at him behind his back. He'd stop people on the street to say, "Merry Christmas," or stagger into the stores to wish the clerks the same but they would just shy away from him. After Gunnar and the cook had left, Halldór sat in front of the wood stove with his feet up on the oven door. It was so quiet that when the spruce firewood snapped, it startled him. He could hear his alarm clock ticking. His heart was like a steady drumbeat. "Why does it keep beating?" he wondered.

He thought he would make coffee, but then changed his mind. A field mouse ran out from under the cupboard, another one chased it. He moved his foot and they ran back to hide under the edge of the cupboard. Sometimes, after supper, they became so bold that they searched under the table for crumbs even though he was busy cleaning up.

He tried to look out the window but the inside was covered in ice. He rubbed on it until a small space was clear. The snow was falling in large, soft flakes. Soon the sheds, the tractor, the caboose, would be nothing but mounds of snow. He opened the door and the cold air swirled in.

"Hello!" he shouted. "Anybody but me here?" His voice was muted by the snow.

Sometimes, when he went to town, women had come back with him, but it never lasted. It was too lonely at the camp. There were too many meals to make and too many dishes to wash and little to do except play cards or read. He never expected any woman to stay, so he never wanted to get too close.

He put on his parka and his toque. He pulled on his mukluks. "You can't see your hand in front of your face." That's what his mother used to say on days like this when he was going out to deliver newspapers. It was no time to go out. People got lost going from the house to the barn. Someone would find them when the snowdrifts melted in the spring. He picked up his rifle, stroked the wooden butt, then tucked it under his arm.

The snow enveloped him. After five steps, he couldn't see the cabin. He'd had this dream before. In it he was always standing in a blizzard, unsure of where he was, and a white wolf appeared, baring her fangs.

GYPSY CLOTHES

One day, God was to come to see Eve's children. In preparation for the visit, she was washing them. Before she finished, He appeared. She showed him those who had been washed. He asked her if she did not have more children. Ashamed of those who were still unwashed, she said no, that she had shown all there were. Angry with her for lying, he said, "Let those you have hidden from me remain hidden." From that time there were two classes of people. Those who could be seen and those who could not. Those who could not be seen were called the *huldufólk*. Some called them elves but they were not elves like the elves in Ireland.

These hidden people are just like us, except handsomer, more beautiful, better dressed, superior in every way. They live in certain rocks and cliffs. Many a shepherd or shepherdess, alone in the mountains, or travelling the lonely tracks to the summer meadows, has seen them. There are many stories about these encounters. Some good. Some bad.

After the Icelanders came to Canada, there were discussions about whether any of the other folk—the trolls, rock giants, elves, the devil himself—had come with them. Some said it was impossible, but others claimed to have seen passengers on the sea voyage to Ameríka who briefly appeared but had not been seen again. Others said food had disappeared, and that there had been strange, inexplicable events on the ships.

Not all the immigrants were poverty-stricken. There were a few who, having escaped the worst of the volcanic eruptions, had sold their farms and come with money to buy land and cattle. One of these was a farmer named Gísli. He settled west of Lundi on good land with few stones. A creek ran through his property and it was full of fish in the spring during the spawning. He could take his boat to the Icelandic River and from there to Lundi and, if he wished, out onto the open lake and sail to Gimli or Selkirk or even Winnipeg. His land had on it good timber for building and even open meadows instead of scrub bush or swamp. However, this story is not about him.

He had two daughters, Jónina and Kristín. Jónina was the elder, and a great favourite of her mother because she looked like her. Kristín was quite beautiful but instead of having fair skin and ash blonde hair, she had raven's hair and raven's eyes. Her mother was often heard to say that she must have been a changeling, because it was known the elves, at times, wished their children to be mortal and would trade newborn babies in the crib if one didn't watch closely enough.

Gísli soon had a fine herd of dairy cows, and since dairy products were the main part of the immigrant's diet, they were prized and well taken care of. Jónina preferred indoor work—knitting, sewing, cooking—and Gísli was often away selling and buying various goods so tending the cattle fell to Kristín.

On this farm there was a rise, and on the rise there was a field of large stones. These were covered in moss and interspersed with scrub oak. Nothing grew there except the oak and grass and some wild flowers. There was no other place like it in the district, and no one there could explain where such a field of stone could come from. A trail ran around the field because no one would walk through it.

It was the custom for the family to go to church in Gimli on Christmas Eve. The way was long and, if there had been a lot of snow, the journey difficult. They would have to leave on Christmas Eve morning. They would visit during the day. The service was held in the late evening. If the weather were clear, they would return home in the early hours of the next morning. However, if the weather were bad, they could be delayed not just for hours but for days. Blizzards in Manitoba had claimed many lives when people and horses had become lost.

The Christmas Kristín was sixteen the weather was threatening. Grey, heavy clouds lay low in the sky.

"Someone will have to stay," her mother said. Normally, it would have been the hired man or hired girl, but they had left earlier to be with their families. The previous day, because the weather had been mild, the skies clear, letting them go had seemed reasonable. The winter storms usually didn't begin in earnest until January. There was just enough snow for the sleigh to move easily on the surface.

"We can't risk the cattle going unmilked," Kristín's mother said.

Kristín protested. She, too, had looked forward to visiting, to seeing her friends, to attending the service, to receiving her parish gift.

In Iceland, to leave a young woman alone on Christmas Eve would have been considered a grave risk; but here, in the New World, no one had reported seeing the elves. Those who said the elves had not followed the emigrants seemed to be correct. There was no place for them here where there were no high cliffs, no mountains, no glaciers, so Kristín's parents left her behind. The snow held off. It was likely her family would return at three or four in the morning. After they returned, they would sleep, then have their Christmas dinner and celebration.

She fed the sheep and milked the cows, then began preparing the food for the next day. It was late when she looked out and saw it had begun to snow. The flakes were heavy and soon it was difficult to see as far as the barn. A wind came up. She was putting some sticks of poplar on the fire when there was a knock at the door. She was startled but went immediately to see who was there. A man stood on the steps holding a child's hand.

"We've lost our way," he said. "We were going to visit friends not far from here. May we have shelter?"

She wasn't sure about letting a stranger into the house when she was alone, but the night was cold and the wind bitter. She opened the door and let them in. When they had taken off their outer garments and were sitting by the stove, the child said, "I'm hungry."

Kristín had spent the day cooking *rúllupylsa* and *svið*, making *kleinur* and *pönnukökur* and finishing up some *vínarterta*. The house was filled with the smell of good food. Kristín hesitated, not out of meanness, but because her mother was known to keep a lock on the food cupboard. There had been more than one traveller who, unless he was of some importance, had had to make do with a glass of milk thinned with water and a piece of dry bread with no butter.

Kristín sliced some *hangikjöt* from the bottom so it would not show and took some pieces from the sliced *rúllupylsa*. She put it on a piece of brown bread. She gave the child a glass of milk and was going to make coffee to serve the father when he said, "There are others, but we were unsure of our welcome." He stood up and went to the door. He opened it and out of the storm came one person after another, stamping his or her feet to get the snow off, taking off coats and shawls and hats and piling them up until the house was full of laughing, talking people.

They had all been travelling together to a celebration. They had brought a feast with them and now set it out around the house. Those who had brought musical instruments began to play. They danced and sang until just before midnight, then fell quiet while the man who had first come recited a prayer and gave a benediction, but it was not a prayer or benediction Kristín had ever heard before.

With the crowd had come a woman in fine clothes, and with her was a boy a bit older than Kristín. Kristín would have spoken to him, but with the clamour and the crowding and her own shyness, she did not manage it. She stared at him and he at her, but when he caught her looking at him, she ducked her head and blushed.

When the benediction was over, Kristín said, "I must look to the cows. They must not be forgotten."

She was tending the cattle when she heard the barn door open. It was the tall, handsome man who had first come to ask for shelter. "You're very beautiful," he said. "Let me make love to you."

"I think not," she said. "Is it that you want to marry me?"

He had a silver tongue and heaped compliments upon her, thanking her for her hospitality and kindness, but she'd heard words like these before from other men, so she recited the Lord's Prayer to herself to keep out the words of his flattery and tended to the cattle. Finally, he went away. In a few minutes the door opened again but this time it was a woman.

"I've been outside listening," she said. "Thank you for refusing my husband. You will be a faithful and loyal wife for some fortunate man. Come with me."

They went out into the snowstorm to the sleighs that stood between the barn and the house. The woman opened a trunk. "Virtue may be its own reward," she said, "but it's sweeter when there's something else as well. You'll have missed out on the Christmas gift at the church so here is something for you."

She gave Kristín a package and told her to put it under her bed until she was by herself.

"We are of a similar shape and size," she said. "I'll give you some of my fine clothes. No one but you will be able to wear them and you are not to wear them until after you've come from the church on your wedding day."

They went back to the house together and Kristín did as she was told. The entertainment had grown quiet and the music now was meant for listening. It made Kristín think of sunsets and sunrises, of summer skies, of happiness and sadness, of an aching longing for someone to love.

The storm had eased and, gradually, the visitors went away. At last the house was empty and Kristín fell into a deep sleep. When she awoke, the house was much as it had been because her guests had taken their belongings with them.

She retrieved the gift package from under the bed. When she laid the items out, there was a beautiful embroidered dress, a fur cloak with velvet lining, and fur-lined boots. There was everything anyone would need for winter travelling.

The snow began again and held for three days. She took care of the cattle and the house and wondered if she would spend the winter alone. At last the sky cleared and her parents and sister came into the yard in their sleigh.

"We thought you might have died in the storm," her mother said. "Your father was worried about what would have happened to the cattle."

Kristín told them little about the night except that some lost travellers had taken refuge with her and, in return for their shelter, had given her some gifts. Her mother slapped Kristín's face for allowing strangers into the house and then went to check to see that no item had been stolen. She demanded Kristín show her the gifts that she'd been given. Kristín reluctantly showed her mother the gifts. Although Kristín protested and tried to stop her, Jónina took the jacket to try on. Although it looked large enough for her to wear when she held it up, when she tried to put it on she found it too small. The harder she tried to force her arms into the sleeves, the narrower they became.

"You'll never get into these on your wedding day," her sister said and flung them onto the floor.

The story of the visitors went around the community. Many neighbours came to see the gifts. No one knew who the visitors might be. Some thought that they must have been gypsies because of the brightly embroidered clothes. Some tried to get Kristín to model them but she always replied that she'd wear them after being to church on her wedding day. When no one was able to find out who the visitors were, the rumour went around the community it had been the elves who had visited.

The next year on Christmas Eve morning, her mother insisted she would stay at home while the others went to church. She said Kristín had missed out on the visiting and the service and a gift the year before. She didn't want her to go two years in a row without taking Christmas communion.

The family's return was delayed because of a broken runner on the sleigh and they did not arrive home until late the following morning. The windows of the farmhouse were dark.

When they let themselves in, the fire was out. There was frost on the inside of the windows. Kristín's mother was lying on the floor. She could not move. They carried her to bed.

"What happened?" her husband asked. They had planned that if any visitors came, she would receive them with great hospitality and, in return, receive bountiful gifts.

When she spoke, the words were jumbled and often did not make any sense. Once she was able to get up and move around, she used gestures and pantomime with occasional words to make them understand that a shabbily dressed man and a child had come to the door saying that they had lost their way. Because of the beauty and elegance of the clothes given to Kristín, she was expecting visitors dressed like kings and queens. She'd been reluctant but finally agreed to let them in to get warm. There was food on the table but she saw no need to give them anything because it was obvious they were nothing more than beggars.

The child began to cry and asked if she could have something to eat. Her father asked if she, at least, might have something to drink. Kristín's mother gave her a glass of water with some whey. The child's father said his daughter had not eaten in a long time. Kristín's mother said no, everything that was prepared was already meant for others. The child reached out to take a piece of bread and Kristín's mother struck her so hard across the face that the child's nose began to bleed. The child cried bitterly. Her father picked her up and carried her out the door.

"They came back?" her husband asked. She nodded in reply. Although her body healed, she never was the same again. She dragged one leg and the arm on the same side was weak. It was a long time before she was able to knit but once her strength came back enough she would sit in her rocking chair with her needles and wool. Any time someone came to the farm door, she would flee to her room and stay there until the visitor had gone.

The summer Kristín was nineteen, she met a blond young man on the path that went around the field of stones. He was, he said, visiting some relatives and, if she would let him, he'd walk the rest of the way with her. She thought she'd seen him before and asked him if they hadn't met, perhaps at a wedding or a funeral. He said that they hadn't met but, perhaps, one time before when he was visiting, they'd caught sight of each other. He bent down and picked her a bouquet of wild daisies. After that, he came often to the farm. His name was Böðvar and he knew enough stories from times past to entertain her for a lifetime. He also had plans for the future. They were married four months later in December. After the wedding, Kristín changed into her fine clothes meant for winter travelling. They were not at all like what local women wore but they made her more beautiful than ever. The guests marvelled at the cloth and the fine stitching.

No one could agree on who might have designed the clothes. Some still thought it was gypsies, others said Galicians or Russians. Some thought it might be Germans because there was a colony of them to the west. An old woman whispered it was the elves but she was soon hushed, because people said this was a new land and there was no need for the old beliefs, that it was gypsies, truly, because who else could be both so generous and so cruel. They said Kristín's mother simply had a stroke.

Whoever they were will never be known, because they never came back. However, it is known that on the day of Kristín's wedding, she insisted on walking with her new husband through the snow to the stone field in her gifted clothes and stood there on the rise. Some said she wanted to look one last time at the view because she was going west, all the way to British Columbia, and would never return, but others said it was not like that at all. Instead of taking in the view, she stood, and twirled and curtsied as if she was showing off her finery to an invisible audience.

The field of moss-covered stones is still there on the ridge, the scrub oak is still gnarled and stunted, but something changed when Kristín and her husband left. The sunlight no longer fell so richly in winter and summer on the field, there was no longer a sense of something special, something not seen but felt. The flowers do not bloom in such profusion. Many people, at one time, used to go by this place, but no longer. It is said the *huldufólk* left with Kristín and her husband, that they wanted to be where they were welcome and where, once again, there would be mountains and the sea would be close.

Kristín's father and mother moved to Gimli. The farm fell into disrepair. The back of the barn broke and sagged. The house went unpainted. The fields grew over again with poplar.

Those who believed in the elves said when the elf-man came to the barn to tempt Kristín with flattery, he was testing her to see if she would be a suitable wife for his son. How else could the elf-woman know Kristín would have a winter wedding?

Kristín, in spite of the prophecy she would never return, did come to visit her mother in the nursing home, Betel, and, later, to visit her father there. She brought her children each time, but could not stay long because there was much to do in their farm at the coast. She lived a long life, she and her husband prospered, and when she finally died, she was greatly missed.

THE NEW WORLD

The new world was a strange place for both the settlers and those who came with them. Just as humans do, ghosts and trolls and *huldufólk* have need of places to live. The ghosts lived alone and so did most of the trolls, though some of the trolls had wives and some troll couples had children. The *huldufólk*, those others who were most like humans, lived in a parallel, invisible world, in prosperous communities with both leisure and time for social lives. In Iceland, dancing was banned; but the *huldufólk* loved to dance and even the *huldufólk* bishops joined in the parties. The *huldufólk* farmed hay and kept cattle, but did it so well they never went hungry. They had many excellent smiths, carpenters, and cobblers. They wore fine clothes and ate good food. Hearths with good driftwood logs kept them warm all year around.

The trolls, ghosts, and *huldufólk* all came with the immigrants, because it was not just land that held them, but people. What is a troll, or a ghost, or one of the invisible people, without humans? They all crowded onto ships and followed their humans through foreign streets. Although they knew about the *jöklar* and the fjords, the heaths and barren sand deserts of Iceland, the fertile valleys and the rivers rich with salmon, they had no more knowledge of vast forests or open prairies than the settlers themselves.

Where were they to shelter in Nova Scotia or Ontario or Manitoba? These were poor places for these others who were used to finding homes in precipitous cliffs and lava caves.

There were new opportunities, but deer and moose eluded clumsy attempts to hunt them. Regret came easily as winter winds howled and snow drifted roof high or higher. Immortality does not exclude suffering and the *huldufólk* suffered. They were no more adept at using an axe to fell trees than were any of the settlers.

Trolls found places. One lived under a bridge outside of Arborg. Another sheltered in a den at Narcisse until it filled with snakes. He fled in terror because there are no snakes in Iceland, but he could find no other place to live; so he returned, and while the snakes slept, he spent the winter eating them. He ate them, head first, holding them by the tail. They didn't taste like fish or sheep or even people, but it was not a bad taste and he soon grew used to it.

The ghosts had the least problems, because they slept with their people and those that still ate found something to live on. The ghosts were quick to realize rabbits were plentiful. They helped themselves to animals caught in traps. A trapper knew they'd been there when all there was in a trap was a foot, or when a trap had been sprung but no animal was in it. However, the ghosts suffered because in the New World the reasons they walked no longer existed. It was difficult to nurse their anger or pain in the forest or field with nothing to remind them of the reason for their anger or sorrow. Soon some of them forgot why they walked. Their sense of injustice ebbed but the graves they would have returned to were half a world away.

What does a ghost do when it no longer has reason to exist? A few managed to follow the Icelanders who returned to Iceland, but most Icelanders remained in the New World. The ghosts sometimes sat on drift logs on the lakeshore. On a calm day, when the surface of Lake Winnipeg was smooth but small waves curved at the edge and broke on the sand, people said the sound was that of the ghosts weeping.

The *huldufólk* fared the best. They were smarter, stronger, had more resources. They adapted more quickly and, in their parallel world, cleared land and produced crops sooner than the settlers. They marvelled at what could be done with the land and revelled in the grain that could be grown. Bread was no longer a luxury. Meat replaced dried fish heads. Here, there was all the fuel they could wish. They no longer had to dry fish bones for burning. Nor did they need to cut turf that smouldered and filled their houses with smoke. In Iceland, only the Danish merchants could afford to have birch firewood brought on the trade ships. In the New World, any man could cut birch or spruce for his stove, and where in Iceland there had only been stoves in the Danish traders' homes, here there were stoves for everyone.

Some *huldufólk*, it is true, suffered from homesickness. There were no great cliffs and fjords. No glaciers shone in the summer light. *Huldufólk* are literate and they often wrote poetry about their longing for the fjords, the waterfalls, the great ice mountains, but they also remembered how the humans they came with had suffered from hunger and cold and injustice.

Soon, the *huldufólk* suffered from a breakdown of social order. For centuries, everything had followed a pattern. Now, knowledge was new for everyone.

"We are too few," some complained. "We are without company, without society." To remedy this, they decided that they would entice human children to join them. Two children disappeared, but it was the wolves humans blamed, because wolves, being curious creatures, watched humans at work. Wolves were seen as they lay at the edge of the forest. A child was put outside in a bassinette. He disappeared without a trace. Another child went to play beyond the cleared ground and was not seen again.

A third child, though, a boy of six named Gissur, disappeared while berry picking. Neither blood nor bones were found. His small pail partly full of saskatoons was sitting on a rock.

Weeks passed and then he reappeared, stumbling into the yard in a daze. When his parents asked him where he had been, he didn't reply but simply stared at them open-mouthed. Before he had disappeared, he had talked well; but now he did not speak, pointing at anything he wanted, shaking or nodding his head, watching everyone with suspicion, as if they were strangers.

When he was pleased, he neither smiled nor laughed, and when he was hurt, he didn't cry. Always, he stayed a distance away from everyone else, always watching. When others said their prayers at night, he closed his eyes and said nothing.

"Bewitched," people whispered. "Something's taken his mind." But Gissur's mind was fine. He was as quick to help as before, even more so, for he'd given up children's games. Instead, he followed the adults around, watching and doing what they did. When his father got into his skiff to row to his nets, Gissur climbed in with him and took a seat at the front. When his father took fish from the nets, Gissur watched him intently, missing nothing, then, picking up the small hook used for freeing the mesh, began to pull fish loose. Yet, his parents did not like to leave him alone, because he often drifted into waking dreams in which he heard or saw nothing that went on around him.

"He's grown old," some of the neighbours said. "He's an elf changed for a child. When he's alone, he'll talk to himself and reveal that he's an elf. Then beat him until he confesses and make him bring your child back."

His parents listened and watched but their son did not talk to himself. He sat at the table watching first one, then the other. He studied his brothers and sisters and they, being studied, looked away. It was as if he'd come from another world and was filled with curiosity about this one.

"He's so serious," his mother said. "He leans forward to listen to every word when his father reads the Bible. I offered him a *kleina*. It was always his favourite treat. He took it but he never smiled. A *kleina* always used to make him smile."

There were no reasons to complain about his behaviour. If the other children had behaved as well, many parents would have been pleased. But his watching unnerved them. "Why does he come to stare at me," the blacksmith complained. "I feel like he's looking right through me. It's like he knows all my secret thoughts."

When he was older, he got out of bed one morning and went to his mother and hugged her and when she hugged him back, he smiled.

"Where have you been?" she asked. "It's like you haven't been here."

"Away," he said. "I went with the elves. Ever since I came back, I wasn't sure you were real." He touched her face. "I thought you were a dream. They wanted me to stay."

"But you did come back."

"It was hard," he said. "They had fine clothes and food and they said that I would live forever."

Because she was afraid he'd change his mind and join the elves again and never return, his mother kept close watch over him. In a while he was more like he had been before he had disappeared, but he was never the same. He'd become more watchful, less certain of everything around him; he wrote poetry and stories, he daydreamed, he never quite joined in community events, even when he was older and young men were courting. He stood aside at dances and parties, always watching, and he only married because one young woman watched him watching everyone else and gently took his hand and married him. He studied her as if he were uncertain, at times, that she was real, but she didn't mind. People said there was something odd about her as well, as if she, too, had been bewitched in childhood.

One time when he and she were together, they were passing by some limestone cliffs in their boat. She would have had him land because blueberry bushes grew there but he refused and would go no closer.

"I've been there," he said. He pointed to a large cleft in the rock. "The area is dangerous with reefs. I went there one time when I was very young."

Gissur and his wife eventually went to Winnipeg. There he became a scholar. He studied philosophy and wrote many essays and books on reality, on the seen and the unseen, on the sixth sense, on perception and human limitations.

He wrote a verse that said:

When I was young, I visited the elves
They resemble nothing so much as ourselves
Except they hold the key
To immortality.

It is said that gradually, the *huldufólk* gave up their plan to increase their numbers and, because they lived in a better place, they let more of their children join human society and become mortal. Their children joined in marriage with humans and had children. These children were fair-skinned with hair so blond it was nearly white. They could be seen most often at Íslendingadagurinn. They inherited a love of beauty, art, and writing, and had about them a tendency to be lost in thought, as if they could see a world invisible to others. If someone asked them what they were seeing, they'd say, "Oh, nothing. Just daydreaming," but their smile was always wistful, as if they had been looking at a world that was gradually fading and would soon disappear.

QUARANTINE

There was a good woman who, with her husband and children, came with the settlers. Her name was Guðný Ólafsdóttir. She knew her history and a few other things as well. When the smallpox began in Gimli, Guðný Ólafsdóttir said it might have come in the blankets sent from Montreal. Many nodded in agreement. There would have been few who did not know about the great plague of 1493 that was brought by English merchants to Hafnarfjörður. It came in cloth they'd brought to sell. The disease was so terrible people died even as they milked their cows. When mourners went to bury the dead, sometimes only half of them returned home alive.

There was, Guðný reminded people, another similarity. When the plague began it was not so bad in the warmer weather but, as the days grew cold, it became more and more deadly. The same was true in Gimli. Like Torfi of Klofi, she said, we should flee to a better place. The difference was that Torfi was able to take his family and farmhands to a distant valley in the interior of Iceland before the plague reached his farm. Nor was there anyone to stop him.

Once it was known there was smallpox in New Iceland, the government authorities quarantined all of the colony. It was impossible to flee. No one was allowed to cross Netley Creek. Money within the colony was very short and the supplies that could be bought were brought to the creek and left on the bank where the colonists could retrieve them. Although a watch was kept, the supplies were sometimes stolen.

Guðný was not the sort to remain idle. When she had first arrived in Toronto, she had taken work as a domestic. When the group of Icelanders with whom she'd emigrated decided to leave for what was then the North West Territories (Manitoba was so small it was called the postage-stamp province), she did not hesitate.

She had managed to come to Canada by borrowing thirty dollars. She had paid off one third of it by scrubbing floors in Winnipeg. She had returned to New Iceland just before the smallpox broke out.

In Iceland she had washed wool, carded it, and spun it. In Iceland, she and her husband had knitted; even the children had a daily quota, because everyone needed mitts, socks, and underwear for their own use and then more to trade. In Canada, she never rested without knitting needles in her hands, because there was always someone who would pay five or ten cents for well-knitted mittens.

She was used to making shoes from sheepskin, but now, when she saw the natives wearing moccasins made from tanned deer hide, she asked them to teach her to do that.

It was thought the quarantine would last only a short time, but as the winter progressed, it became apparent it would not be lifted for many months. The settlement was in desperate need of medical supplies.

Not only could the settlers not flee to a new area, they could not even isolate the sick. They had only been able to build as many cabins as they had stoves and those were few. Guðný tended her own family and she also nursed the sick. Because only a dozen households were not affected, there were many to be nursed.

The winter turned bitterly cold. The temperatures dropped to forty degrees below zero. There was heavy snow. The ground was as hard as the lava fields they'd left behind. There was no burying the dead. Instead,

Guðný helped lay them out and wrap them in canvas. So the animals could not eat them, the bodies were laid side by side on the roofs of the cabins.

"We should never have come," one old man said. "We should have stayed home and been buried in Iceland's soil."

Another said, "They told me I was a traitor when I left and that I would regret my decision."

The cabins were crowded. Outside, the forest was thick and tangled. The drifted snow was piled high. The lake they had hoped would feed them was locked under four feet of ice. All the way to the horizon there was nothing but a white, dangerous wilderness.

"The land of opportunity," another said bitterly. "We were going to eat until we burst."

They were trapped there, struggling to survive against disease, cold, and lack of food. These were bitter times. Guðný went to one cabin only to find both parents dead, the cabin freezing, and two children huddled beside their mother.

"We must have medical supplies," she said. She went from person to person, collecting five cents here, ten cents there.

There had been a road cut through the bush as far south as Boundary Creek. She walked this trail, starting so she would arrive late at night. She passed through the camp where the men who were cutting the trail were living. She prayed there'd be no wind, that the snow would not begin to drift, that she'd not lose her way in the dark. She crossed the creek like a dark shadow, and then walked until she was well beyond the quarantine boundary. That night, she took her sheepskins from her sled, laid them on the snow, wedged a pole between two small trees and draped a piece of old canvas over it. She covered herself with a horsehide. When she woke, it was still dark and she was shivering with cold. She was on the edge of some forest when she saw, across an open field, travellers on a sleigh. She waited in the shadows and watched as the sleigh came toward her. Explaining where she had come from was going to be impossible, so she turned around and began to walk back the way she had come.

When they caught up to her, they ordered her to stop and questioned her. She said she'd left Winnipeg, where she'd been working, and that she was returning to Gimli. The three men, who worked for the government, ordered her to return to Winnipeg and stay there until the epidemic was over.

She did turn south, except that she went to Selkirk. There she found shelter with a cousin who'd been vaccinated in Iceland and so was not afraid of the pox.

"They say that before spring they'll all be dead," her cousin said.

"The devil makes his rounds," Guðný answered, thinking of her husband and children. "I wish I could fly like the birds."

She walked thirty miles to Winnipeg. Three Icelandic women who were working in the city, cleaning houses, took her in. Their only furniture was a table and one chair. They took turns sitting in the chair and they all slept on the floor. The next day, she shopped for the supplies that were so desperately needed. The weather had turned cold and clear. The three women tried to persuade her to stay.

"The wolves will follow you," one said. "When we came to Winnipeg in late summer, they flitted in and out, watching to see if one of us would fall behind."

"Árni from Vopnafjörður lost his way," another said.

They all knew that story. A wind had come up and the drifting snow blotted out all landmarks. He walked all night and all day on the ice and died a mile from Hnausa. The wolves had found his body first. All they left was blood, scattered bones, and torn clothing.

In a Manitoba winter, the coldest, most desperate part of the day is in the hours before dawn. Guðný dressed early, drank coffee, and waited. When the sky began to lighten, she started her journey back. She could hear trees crack from the cold. The glare from the snow made her eyes sore. She rested at Lower Fort Garry and warmed herself at a stove. She'd brought bread and cheese and a piece of dried fish in her pocket.

When she began walking again, she was already weary. She had hoped she might get a ride on a sleigh but none of the English would offer a ride. The Icelandic women who worked in Winnipeg had been told that when they were out, they were not to look English people in the face. They were to keep their eyes downcast. They were not to speak unless spoken to first. No Icelanders went by. At Selkirk, she stopped at her cousin's house again.

"I don't like the look of the clouds," her cousin said in the morning. The clouds were grey and ribbed and hung low in the sky.

"They're waiting," Guðný said, thinking of those who were ill, all crowded together, praying for her return. She packed her supplies into her sled

She walked, after a while, as if she were in a dream, as if there were a separate person and then there were this body that kept moving forward. What she wished for was no more than a stopping place, a piece of floor and some warmth. The forest was full of shadows. The clouds pressed down upon her.

That night, she made herself a small fire in a place where others had stopped. They'd tramped down the snow and left a pile of fresh spruce branches they'd used as a bed. As she was sitting at the fire, a shadow moved among the trees. She wondered if it was a wolf, but then a man appeared. He was tall and had a narrow face and a fur hat. She pointed to the fire. He came and sat on his haunches. The fire played on his face.

"Do I know you?" she asked.

"A little," he replied. "Not as well as some." He put another branch on the fire. "You're hungry?"

"A little," she admitted. "I've eaten nothing but hardfish for supper." She was drinking cold coffee from a jar she'd carried inside her coat so it wouldn't freeze.

"You're cold," he said.

"A little," she agreed, "since I've stopped walking. The frost finds its way in."

"Would you like a warm room with a good fireplace and a table with hot fish soup, lamb stew, and bread with all the butter you could eat?" He had a walking stick resting across his knees. He took it in his right hand and struck the ground. Immediately, the ground opened up at Guðný's feet and there was a room as he'd described.

"Everything has a price," he said. "Let me have what you carry under your dress and you can spend the night sleeping before this fireplace and, in the morning, take with you as much as your sled will carry."

She did not reply immediately but stared into the fire. "I think not," she said. "I know that old game. If I'm to have a child, I'll keep it for myself."

"You are wiser than most," he said and struck the ground again. The opening closed and where it had been was nothing but snow and ice. "You wished that you might fly like a bird." As he held out his walking stick, it turned into the thighbone of a horse. "You can ride this."

She half-smiled. "When I was young, I had many suitors. Many were braggarts," she said. "I know that kind."

"I have no need to brag," he said and there was an edge of hurt vanity in his voice.

"Show me how big you can make yourself then," she said. He made himself large and monstrous, like a great, tormented shadow. "Now, make yourself small as a moth."

When he hesitated, she laughed and waved one hand as if to dismiss him. His face twisted with anger, but then a moth fluttered in the air. She'd been pushing a burning stick further into the fire. In an instant, she touched the moth. It burst into flames and fell into the flames.

She took the walking stick to help her keep her footing on the icy path. She was alone when she met the devil's handyman but, somehow, the story of their meeting began to circulate. The cane was strange, not like anything the Icelandic settlers had seen because it had been cut from diamond willow, the bark peeled away and the wood rubbed with clear oil. The settlers who saw it said in the twisted shapes of the willow they could see some of the ancient runes.

Before the smallpox was over, she made two more trips to Winnipeg. The way was hard and lonely, the path narrow, the temptations many because the weather was so cold frost encrusted the trees, and the tops of the snowdrifts were polished by the wind until they were hard.

The devil's handyman never approached her again, but she knew he was there, lurking in the shadows. She made herself not wish for that which she could not have so he could not tempt her. She knew as she trudged over the snow or huddled before a small fire that he was always waiting to offer her something that otherwise was unobtainable.

Some said she was clever, and that is why she did not get caught leaving or returning to the quarantine area; but others said it was because she rode the devil's walking stick. There was talk she must be a witch and no one denied it. Those for whom she had brought medicine and supplies said she practised only white magic, and like Sæmundur when he tricked the devil into taking him across the sea, she used her power for the benefit of others. There still lingered in the dark crevices of some minds old stories about the burnings, but most saw the possibilities of good soil and a lake full of fish. The way would be hard but there was a way ahead and they had only time for opportunity, not envy.

The stick hung on her kitchen wall for a long time, but then one of her children took it down without permission. He tried to fly it, but instead broke it and threw it into the stove to hide what he had done.

WINDIGO

They say the devil lurks in corners; but more often, it seems, he makes mischief within the human heart. In spite of their travails, some of the settlers in the early years of New Iceland found it impossible to work together. Even though there were trees to be cut, fields to be cleared and planted, swamps to be drained, houses to be built, and cattle to be cared for, people spent most of their time arguing. Instead of working together, they folded their arms, thrust out their bottom lips, and narrowed their eyes at their neighbours. Stones that needed more than one man to move lay in the fields. Bridges that needed building went unbuilt. Houses and barns that needed a whole community to put up were nothing but piles of logs.

Instead of working together, they argued over the correct length of a minister's frock coat, the proper procedure for smoking fish, whether to plant seeds by the light of the moon or the sun. If this did not make life difficult enough, a spirit named Windigo lived nearby in the forest. Although the settlers had come to a new land and had thought to escape all that plagued them in the old country—rock giants, trolls, hunger, poverty, the devil in all his forms, Grýla and her offspring—disease and hunger waited for them.

In the dark, endless forests, they heard of this new spirit, a fearsome cannibal as terrible as any they had ever faced. No one had seen him, but all had heard his name whispered. Windigo was bigger than any man in all of Manitoba. He was so big it took four bear pelts to make him a winter cloak.

One winter afternoon as the sun faded and the wind blew from the north and the ice began to shift, Farmer Bjarni said to Jón Litli, "Can you not hear that? That's Windigo grinding his teeth."

Jón was called Jón Litli because his father had been called Big Jón. Since Big Jón had become mixed up in Quebec and had gone south instead of west and had never been seen since, Jón might have been called Big Jón or even Jón except his mother always called him Jón Litli at the top of her voice whenever he managed to get out of her sight. She'd taken her eyes off Big Jón for just a moment and he'd disappeared. She wasn't going to have it happen to Jón Litli. If Big Jón had not disappeared, Jón Litli and his mother would not have had to live on charity. Other members of the community would not have had to share their turnips, potatoes, and fish.

Sometimes in the gathering dusk, although there was no wind, the trees would start to sway and people would yell, "Windigo is coming!" Children panicked. Mothers panicked. Fathers panicked. The mayor of the town, a little man with a large moustache, took out his trumpet and played three loud blasts. When they heard the warning, everyone scurried inside and locked their doors.

"What should we do?" Jón Litli asked.

"Run," his mother said, grabbing him by the hand. She dragged him under an overturned boat.

People hid in the barns, they hid under the beds, they hid in the root cellars, they hid in haystacks. Some said if he caught them, Windigo ate children, bones and all. Some said he ate them raw and some said cooked. In the darkest forest where the sun never penetrated, there was an enormous cave where he kept children and fed them cookies and cakes and tarts and candy until they were fat and juicy and ready for the spit. Some children who had nothing to eat but one small dried fish a day tried standing out where they would be sure to be seen, but their parents dragged them into a hiding place.

Windigo wore his hair in one long braid. It hung down to the ground and with a snap of his head, he could wrap his braid around a tree and jerk the tree from the ground, or snap his braid around a cow's neck and jerk the cow into his arms. It took the hide of a cow to make him a single shoe.

When people heard what sounded like thunder on a clear day, they knew it was Windigo snoring. He could carry a stolen sheep on each shoulder. He could carry away eight sacks of beans at a time.

One night, when a farmer took a shortcut through the swamp, Windigo caught hold of the back of his sleigh filled with flour. The two oxen struggled but it did no good. Windigo dragged the sleigh backwards into the swamp. The farmer jumped down and ran for his life. That night everyone saw a large fire in the marsh and smelled bread baking and roasting meat. The next spring when the water was low, a hunter found the remains of the wagon and the bones of the oxen.

Windigo's cave, it was said, was filled with a fortune in furs he had stolen from all the trappers he had killed. He carried a hunting knife longer than a scythe and as sharp as a razor. A deer would be leaping through the forest, then Windigo's knife would flash, and three seconds later there would be nothing but steaks and chops and roasts.

One summer's evening just as the sun was going down, even though there wasn't a cloud in the sky, a fisherman saw the surface of the lake ripple and shouted, "Windigo is coming." The baker shouted, "Windigo is coming." The banker would have shouted "Windigo is coming," but there weren't any bankers yet because the people didn't have any money. So, instead, the mayor took out his trumpet and blew three loud blasts. Soon everyone was hiding under beds, in haylofts, under haystacks, in root cellars.

Jón Litli and his mother were hiding under the boat again. They could hear the trees thrash back and forth as he passed. They could hear his heavy, asthmatic breathing that sounded like a sudden, violent wind through the trees.

These were brave people. They said they were not afraid of leaving their homes in Iceland and travelling to a far country like Canada. They said they weren't afraid of the deep, dark forests, even though there were no forests in Iceland. They said they were not afraid of the bears and the wolves, the lynx and the coyotes, even though there were no wild animals like these in Iceland. They said they were not afraid of walking for days on the trails between farms and all the way to Winnipeg to buy flour and rice and carry it back. They said they weren't afraid of starving to death even though the lake froze over and they couldn't fish. They said they weren't afraid of freezing to death even though in Iceland, they'd never felt such cold.

After it was safe to come out, they all gathered around a bonfire to tell of their experience of how close Windigo had come to them, of how they were within an inch, a fraction of an inch, of being discovered and dragged from their hiding places and carried away to be stewed in a huge, black metal pot with turnips and potatoes and onions. Some people said if they were thrown into the pot alive, they'd eat the turnips, potatoes, and onions.

"We can't live like this," the mayor said. "We need a champion to find him, slay him, and bring back his furs for all of us to share."

"I've got crops to plant," one of the farmers said.

"I've got a horse to shoe," the blacksmith said.

"I've got nets to lift," a fisherman said.

"Let us draw straws," the mayor said. "Let fate determine who shall be a hero."

The mayor pulled a handful of straws from a stack, broke them all off even except for one. He held out the straws to each of the men. They all pulled a straw until there was only one left. "And this," the mayor said to Jón Litli, "is yours."

"He's just a boy," Jón Litli's mother said. " Jón Litli can't go travelling. Not for many years yet."

"The straw," ordered the mayor, and Jón Litli reached out for it. This time, the mayor did not hold the straw tight so it could not be drawn from between his thumb and forefinger, as he had done with the others.

"You've been chosen as our champion," the mayor said.

The village folk all cheered, but his mother protested. "You can't send him out by himself. He's just a boy. Windigo will make a snack of him and pick his teeth with his bones."

"You've often said that Jón Litli's *langafi*, way back in the days of the vikings, was a viking's viking," the mayor said. "Not just any viking. The kind whose name made people's knees quake and their faces go pale."

Everyone nodded; for it was true, when Jón Litli's mother felt discouraged, she made up stories about her ancestors. She might have to live on charity because of her husband's poor sense of direction, but she came from a line of kings and warriors. Her great-something-or-other once owned a sword called Leg Biter and, in one battle, he'd killed six men with it. Jón Litli didn't have a sword, but he had a paring knife and a heavy stick with a knot in one end. He'd once used the stick to chase a fox away from his mother's chickens.

"How do you know there's anything to be afraid of?" Jón Litli asked. "Has anyone ever actually seen Windigo?"

"My cousin could tell you how Windigo stole two of his sheep one night in a blizzard but he's not living here anymore," said Bergi from Berstafjell. "He fled to Winnipeg."

"My sister was chased by him once when he wanted a wife," Helga said, "and her hair has gone pure white. She ran and ran and never stopped until she reached North Dakota."

"He sounds like a bully and bullies are all cowards at heart," the mayor said. With that, he borrowed a shawl from one of the women, and then asked for supplies for Jón Litli's adventure.

The village folk donated twelve dried fish, a dozen sugar lumps, four potatoes, two turnips, a beet, and most of a vínarterta. The mayor tied it all up in the shawl. "Don't go looking for trouble," his mother said. "You're all I've got. What will happen to me if he catches you and fattens you up like a pig in a pen, then roasts you for dinner?"

"Will anyone come with me?" Jón Litli asked. "More are greater than one. More are stronger than one." He was going to say, "More are smarter than one," but he'd seen chickens in a flock and wasn't sure that was right.

The only one who spoke was Mrs. Bjarnadóttir, and she said, "I have to stay home to take care of my children." There was no denying that. She had sixteen children and cooked their breakfast porridge in a washtub.

"I'll go myself," Jón Litli replied.

His mother threw her apron over her head and wept. "Woe, woe is me," she said. She had hoped Jón Litli would grow up to become a merchant or a lawyer or a janitor or even a successful cobbler. Now she was looking at years of taking in boarders or doing other people's laundry or working as a servant. "I wish I hadn't told him all those stories about his viking ancestors," she said.

People had a lot of opinions about Windigo. Some knew he lived to the north of town, some knew he lived to the south, some to the west, some to the east. Since the lake bounded the town on the east and Windigo wasn't a fish, Jón Litli decided there was no point searching in that direction.

First, Jón Litli searched to the south. Here, there were long stretches of swamp. The mosquitoes there were as big as hummingbirds. The horseflies were the size of sparrows. Not many people lived in the swamp. A few people had settled there in a dry year and were too stubborn to leave when the water came back.

"Aren't these fields rather wet?" Jón Litli asked of the first farmer he saw. The farmer was standing in water up to his knees.

"They've been wetter," the farmer said. He was building rafts for his sheep so they could float about eating the marsh grass. "Besides, the spring pigs are delicious smoked. Come and help me herd them."

They waded through the swamp, beating the water with sticks. Ahead of them carp as large as year-old pigs swam toward a pen made of saplings.

"Sometimes Windigo goes swimming," the farmer said, "and then things are bad. The water rises and fields flood. I've not seen him, but take this canoe and visit my neighbour. I'm sure he's seen him."

Jón Litli paddled from one neighbour to the other. They fed him fresh fish and let him sleep on their floors at night. At every farm, Jón Litli asked where he could find Windigo. They took him on their boats to show him how when he stole fish from them, Windigo tangled their nets into a ball, how he made great holes in their nets, how, when he was angry, he flung their boats onto the shore. But none of them could actually say they'd seen him. As they all worked digging out stumps and clearing away rocks, cutting wood, scything grass, they all told him of the cave full of furs and how, if they could just find it, they would have everything their hearts desired.

When there was nowhere else to search in the south, Jón Litli turned to the west. The west was all gravel ridges with swamps in between. Sometimes, in the thick tangle of forest, there were long stretches of good soil. Here, farmers had built their log cabins.

As he hiked from farm to farm, Jón Litli was fed smoked sheep's heads and soured milk and given a bed in the haylofts. None of them had seen Windigo but they all could show him where Windigo had been. There was a group of trees he'd knocked over in a rage. There was a field of wheat he'd trampled one night when he'd come to steal chickens. There was the barn roof he'd ripped off. There was evidence everywhere of his passing.

"Try my neighbour," one farmer after the other told Jón Litli.

Gradually, he worked his way toward the north, following the faint trails where the forest was thick, the paths narrow, the clearings few and small. When it was dark, there were just the stars and the moon to guide him and every night wolves howled and coyotes barked and owls hooted.

Jón Litli spent some nights huddled around a small fire and he was afraid. The cabins he did find were lonely and isolated. Some of the people hadn't had a visitor in over a year. Everyone was happy to see him. Many of them wanted him to stay but he explained he had to continue with his quest.

"Stay on the path," one of the farmers warned him. "If you get off it, you'll get lost and you'll never be found."

The farmer hadn't seen Windigo himself but he had heard him while he was searching for a lost cow in the forest. Sometimes, for no reason, the hair on the back of his head stood straight up and then he hid in the thickest bush he could find because he knew Windigo was close.

Jón Litli searched for Windigo amid the trees, in the clearings, along streams. He followed directions from one farm to another. He chewed on his dried fish and ate his vínarterta and shared meals with the farmers and their families. Sometimes, at night, the farmers woke him to say, "Listen. Listen. Can't you hear him moving through the forest?" But all Jón Litli could hear was the wind in the poplars.

Windigo's furs, Jón Litli learned, were piled high in a deep limestone cave. Everyone dreamed of finding them. If a person could take even a sleigh-full, he'd never be poor again.

Windigo's hair changed colour with the seasons. In summer it was pale blond, in fall it was red, in winter it was white. In spring, one person said, it was as green as the leaves on the birch trees. He was a spirit and spirits were unpredictable. That was what was so frightening about him. Everything would be fine, then he would appear and someone would die or a sheep would go missing or a crop would be ruined.

"I'm not afraid of anything else," one of the farmers declared. "Not the winters, not the storms, not the loneliness, not the poverty. It's just him I'm afraid of. Windigo."

Jón Litli searched all that summer and all that autumn. When the first snow began to fall, he returned home. When his mother saw him, she screamed and flung the bread she was kneading into the air because she thought she was seeing a ghost. She'd heard Windigo had caught her son and was wearing his ribs for buttons. When she saw he was really alive, she threw her arms around her son, and said, "Thank the Lord, you've returned safely. There's been word of jobs cleaning fish in Winnipeg. It's not much but some day you may become..." and she stopped. She couldn't think of what he might become if he started out cleaning fish, but it was enough that he was her son and he was home safely. All the other villagers, when they heard Jón Litli had returned, rushed to the house. They gathered around him to see if it were really Jón Litli and not his ghost paying one last visit to the village.

"It's a miracle," Mrs. Bjarnadóttir said. "A miracle," others repeated to each other. They touched and pinched Jón Litli to be sure it was really him.

"You have made a great journey. Did you find his cave?" the mayor asked. Everyone leaned forward to see what Jón Litli had in his pack but when Jón Litli opened it, there were only hazelnuts that he had gathered and some smoked fish that had been given to him.

He was going to tell them Windigo didn't live in the east or the south or the west or the north, that cows died in blizzards, bears and wolves killed sheep and carried them off, that windstorms blew down trees, that hail ruined crops, that foxes stole chickens, that it was lonely living on a farm cut out of the forest, that everyone missed their families, that people became lost, that others became ill and because there was no doctor, they sometimes died, but then he saw how eagerly they leaned forward to hear everything he could tell them.

He remembered how big the forest was and how small he had felt. He remembered how lonely he had been for his mother. He remembered how hungry he often was and how he wondered where he would find his next meal after the last of his fish was eaten. He remembered how afraid he often had been on the windy dark nights and how hard it was not to let his fear overcome him.

"I found signs of him everywhere," he said, "in the west, in the south, in the north. Windigo stole a sheep at one farm and six chickens at another. One night when he drank Fred Finnson's chokecherry wine, we heard him rolling around in a field of wheat. But I never set eyes on him myself. If we're to prosper, we'll have to help each other with our chores. We'll have to put aside our differences and work for our common goals. If we do that, we'll grow strong while he grows old and weak and we won't have to be afraid of him any longer."

"His furs?" the mayor asked hopefully. His coat that had once been thick and warm was now threadbare and his trumpet had a dent in it. His children's sheepskin shoes had holes in them.

Jón Litli shook his head. "He keeps them close," he said. "He's not one to share."

SIDEWALK OF GOLD

Einar married late and when he did, he married a woman from the northwest; and everyone knew that on those most isolated of Icelandic farms, wizards and witches lived, and black magic was practised. Runa came as a young bride with black hair and Irish eyes with their blue-grey irises and dark lashes, instead of blonde hair and blue eyes. She brought with her a wooden trunk and in it a dress finer than any farmer's wife should own. She said it was given to her grandmother by a Spanish sea captain but no one believed that.

She chose a grey horse from her husband's herd and when she came to church, people stared at her and at her grey horse, then glanced sideways, their eyes meeting, then sliding away. A grey horse was a favourite among witches.

She made things worse for herself, of course. On days when she was searching for a lost sheep, instead of reciting passages from the Bible, she watched for the hidden people, for elves and trolls. At night, as they all knitted, they first listened to Einar read from the Bible, but what Runa wanted was for someone to sing *rímur* and for another to tell stories of magicians and the supernatural. They all feared the darkness, but she feared it the least and would sometimes go out to fetch things even though dark had fallen.

When Einar brought Runa back to his farm, she already knew some things, but not black magic. She could tell when the weather was going to turn, she knew when a *fylgja* had arrived, she sometimes knew the future, she saw things others did not see, she was not afraid of demons and trolls, and she sometimes made men ashamed by her fearlessness.

Sometimes there was no butter or *skyr*, sometimes there was no dried cod or pickled lamb. Sometimes they went hungry, but less often than their neighbours, because Einar had no use for brandy and when they took their goods to trade with the Danish merchants, he did not take the free brandy they offered him before the bargaining began.

The farmers and their wives whispered her scythe blades were made from the ribs of men and that was why in good weather, Einar's workers cut their hay so quickly. They said she could command the haycocks to fly into the farmyard. They said she bargained with the devil for her dress with its fine embroidery. They said she traded her soul for it because they could think of no other way anyone could have such a dress.

They considered Einar bewitched. He'd been a bachelor a long time. Many women, seeing his house and hayfields, would have married him; but he went to the Westfjords and brought back a descendant of Irish slaves. They thought she must have sent an *uppvakningur* to make him travel so far for a wife.

Her belly didn't swell right away, and some wondered if Einar and the witch from the Westfjords were really married. Married women were pregnant all the time.

One summer day, when she was searching for a lost sheep and collecting tufts of wool that had snagged on the dwarf birch, she thought she saw something at the bottom of the cliff and, curious, she crept closer, hiding behind rocks. There were rumours thieves who lived in the interior in caves did come to steal sheep, but she did not see thieves. Instead, she saw a man and a woman, dressed in better clothes than she had ever seen. As she watched them, a door in the cliff opened and others came out. They all walked away together, leaving the door slightly ajar. She crept to the door and peeked through the crack. Inside, there was elegant furniture like that she'd seen in the Danish merchants' houses. Rich carpets and lamps that looked as if they were made of gold and silver. She saw a movement inside and pulled away. As soon as the door was shut, it disappeared, and only the dark cliff remained. She knew from the stories she'd heard that such places were filled with gold and silver and precious stones.

She told her husband, but Einar held his finger to his lips and shook his head. She did not speak of it again unless they were alone, away from the farmhouse; but she often walked toward the cliff to see if the shadows might show her where the door had been.

Having proof something more existed, she wanted to know what there was beyond sheep, cows, horses, and fish. She was insatiably curious and always went with Einar to sell their wool, eider down, and salt fish. Unlike their neighbours, because their dogs kept the foxes from their sheep, they never had any fox skins to trade. The holds of the ships were outfitted like stores and she often wondered what it would be like to go to Copenhagen where all these things were available every day; but now, she wanted to know what existed beyond warehouses of coffee and grain. Having seen the door in the cliff, she asked about the book, *Gráskinna, Grey Skin*, but people only stared at her and the priest told her not to speak of it, even though it was supposed to exist at the cathedral schools of Hólar and Skálholt.

Even if she had stopped asking about the magic in these books, the whispering would have continued. She sewed a fine hand and that, some thought, was a gift from the devil. Just as it was when Einar's sheep had more lambs than the neighbours'.

On the farm there was an old woman named Helga. She had lived on the farm all her life. Now, she was bent with age and could do little except card wool. No one knew for certain how old she was, but she had worked for Einar's grandparents, then his parents, and now him. She had lived so long she knew things others no longer knew. Runa plied her with butter and kindness in return for her knowledge.

Einar and Runa had no children until Helga told Runa to stand behind a waterfall and wish for a child. Ten months later, Runa had a son she called Sigurður. He was born with a caul and Helga buried it under the threshold of the house. The caul would ensure Runa could have another child if Sigurður died. Sigurður's hair was black but his eyes were as blue as a mountain pool. He was schooled at home and by a teacher who came to stay two months in the winter. He learned his catechism and was confirmed. Like everyone else, he worked with the animals, harvested hay, and took care of the sheep.

His mother loved him as only a mother with one son can love. She was preparing him to go to Hólar to study. He would learn more than most and he would bring her answers to the secrets Hólar held. Sæmundur the Wise had studied at the Black School and had been trapped there for three years before he tricked the devil and escaped. No one knew now where the Black School was, but there were, it was said, still items left by Sæmundur and others that contained runes and spells. Some of these were secretly studied at the schools.

This is the way it was when the volcanic eruptions occurred. The sky grew so dark you could not see your hand in front of your face. The farm workers barricaded themselves inside and waited, uncertain of their fate. Ash filled the air, lava flowed down their valley; but when the skies became clearer and they were able to go out, they saw a miracle. The landward side of their home field stone fence still stood, and the lava had stopped at the very edge, in places filling up the spaces between the rocks. Runa held her hands to her face and said, "It's a miracle from God." But her neighbours did not agree. Only the devil could have stopped the lava just there after it had covered other farmers' fields. The families whose fields had been destroyed wondered, when they saw where the lava had stopped, what Runa had bargained away for the devil's favour. They did not stop to think about Einar's grazing land that was destroyed or, like them, many of his animals that were dead or dying.

"What of them?" Sigurður asked of the three people who had been with his father's family for years. Like most workers, they had nothing but a quilt, a wooden bowl, a horn spoon, their clothes. They might have a few Danish *rigs* dollars under their pillow to pay for their funeral.

"They'll have to find other places," Einar said. "There is nothing here for them. Grass gives us life and the grass is gone."

Runa said, "Helga and Ingi are too old. No one will take them. Neither of them can walk from farm to farm."

"What will we do?" Sigurður asked his parents. "This will not support all of us."

Welfare was a terrifying last resort for destitute people. Members of the family would be auctioned off not to the highest bidder but to the lowest bidder. Farmers would look over a family and say, "That man looks healthy. I'll keep him for a year for ten crowns from the municipality." Another farmer would say, "I think he can work hard. I'll keep him for only nine crowns." The farmer who would take the least got the welfare case. Then they would bid on the wife and then the children. The family members would go to whichever farmer took payment for them. Some farmers treated such people fairly but others fed them scraps, made them sleep with the animals, and worked them into the grave.

"We should sell what little we have left," Sigurður said to his parents, "and go to Ameríka. I've heard the sidewalks are paved with gold. Everyone lives in a palace."

"We only have enough for one fare," his father said. "If we try to sell our cattle now, our neighbours know we must sell and they will give us little, maybe nothing."

"Go first," Runa said. "Send for us in a year. By that time, everyone will have a place. Don't forget us when you get to Ameríka."

Sigurður hugged his mother and father and said, "I promise, on my soul, I will not forget you. No matter what happens, I will bring you to Ameríka."

"I may yet find the door," Runa said.

Sigurður believed his mother had fallen asleep and dreamt what she had seen, that she'd dreamt of a cave with treasures, because they often told such tales at night. They often talked of the *huldufólk*, God's hidden children, invisible unless they wanted to be seen or did not think anyone was looking. He worried more about trolls, because many people disappeared in the mountains. People taken by the trolls had only ever been seen a few times through the magic of Sæmundur the Wise. The faces of the trolls' victims were hideous, their skin turned blue with bruises.

For his part, her husband Einar wanted her to make bread, not raise the dead. However, she was determined to know about *Gráskinna*. It was filled with spells that would bring power and wealth. Men had been burned at the stake for learning what was in its pages, but that had been a long time ago. Even now that the burnings had stopped, it was still dangerous to ask these questions. Her questions to visitors led to gossip and when she and her husband cut their hay quickly, it was said she could raise the dead and have them work through the night for her. Before dawn, she chanted them back into the grave.

"No one has ever found the *huldufólk's* treasure," Sigurður wanted to say to his mother, but he knew when things were bad, it gave her hope, so he kept silent.

It was a five-slipper walk to the coast. The distance was measured in how many of the untanned fish-skin shoes would wear out before he reached a port.

Sigurður drank water from the streams. He stopped at farms where some people, if they had anything to spare, gave him a piece of dried cod and butter. At other farms he was driven away with curses for being a traitor.

There were no passenger ships that came to Iceland. There was, however, a ship that had come to transport the small Icelandic horses to the mines in Scotland and Wales. The captain of the ship built a partition down the length of the hold. On one side he put horses; on the other, Icelanders. The trip took two weeks.

After he'd been in Ontario a while, Sigurður wrote to his parents to say he was well but that he had not yet found the golden sidewalks nor built a palace. He included what little money he could afford. Because he was good with horses, he was hired to work in Toronto delivering goods with a dray.

His father wrote that some animals had survived the poisoned air and he could catch fish from just off shore now that the islands of ash had drifted away. Many of his neighbours had left for Ameríka, but those who remained saw Runa as the cause of their hardship. The last time she attempted to go to church, women blocked the door.

In Ontario, the immigrant women found work as domestics, but the men muttered among themselves. "We did not come for this, for our wives to be servants in another man's house." Many of the men had been farmers, renting land and animals from wealthier landowners. The cottars had been poor but they'd worked for themselves. They had not had to depend on their wives to support them.

Dissatisfied with having to live among strangers, they sent out four men to find a place that would become New Iceland. When they returned, they said they'd found a place on Lake Winnipeg. It had great fields of grass to feed sheep and the lake was full of fish.

Sigurður went with them—along the Great Lakes, overland, down the river on barges to New Iceland. They were towed into the lake by a steamboat, but when a fall storm threatened, the captain cut them loose and left them to drift ashore. They landed on a sandbar thick with willow. Here they set up ragged tents loaned to them by the Hudson's Bay Company.

"Many," he wrote, "have died of scurvy and cold. The ground is so hard and the snow so deep, we cannot bury them but must wait until spring. I have nothing, I'm afraid, dear mother and father, to send. When the summer comes things will be better."

That spring, he walked south and was hired by a farmer. Then he dug sewer lines in Winnipeg. The banks of the sewer line gave way and six of his crew were buried alive. He took his wages and walked back the sixty miles to Gimli with a sack of flour, some rice, oatmeal, salt, and coffee. What money he had left, he mailed to Iceland.

He finished his log shack and managed to make a stove out of stones and tin. He got work in a saw mill. He was paid in cash and lumber. With the lumber, he built a small skiff. He dried and smoked fish for the coming winter.

His father wrote to say many blamed his mother for their misfortunes, accusing her of making a child ill, of causing a cow to die, of causing a miscarriage. He and Runa and the farm workers who were left kept to the farm.

His mother also included a note warning him to watch for a sending, an *uppvakningur* sent to do him harm. There were those who practised magic secretly. She'd risked going out at night and had seen someone in the graveyard. They could only be there to do harm. Helga had told her if her enemies were not powerful enough to take revenge on Runa, they would attack her son. Helga had been Sigurður's constant companion and nurse when he was a child. He called her Amma Helga. She knew the old runes and some other things and because of her fear for Sigurður, she taught them to Runa.

For Sigurður, there was nothing to be done except fish through the ice or cut wood. He had chosen a piece of property in the bay. His plan was to keep a cow and some sheep and have a boat and some nets.

"Your mother does things she has never done before," Ragnar wrote. "No good can come of it, but she cannot be persuaded otherwise. She fears for you and nothing will stop her."

Sigurður was cutting brush for a road when an animal attacked him. It raced through the bush and leapt at his throat. He fell backwards and could not get up before it was on him again. It would have killed him except a black dog, one of those that had started to follow the bush cutting crew, slammed into it, knocking it sideways. They stood on their hind legs and tore at each other's muzzles. By the time Sigurður was able to struggle to his feet and kill the animal with his axe, the snow was covered in blood. The dog's muzzle and side were torn. It all happened so quickly that no one else had moved.

"I've never seen anything like it," the foreman said. "He ignored the rest of us and picked you out. He'd have killed you in another minute." He went to the animal and turned it over. "What is it?" he asked. "I thought it was a fox but this is not like any fox I've ever seen."

"It is a *skuggabaldur*," one of the Icelandic workmen said. "Its father was a cat and its mother a vixen. They are vicious. In Iceland, they kill the sheep. We hunt them and kill them whenever we can. I didn't think they lived in Ameríka."

"It came a long way to find me," Sigurður said. He turned to look for the black dog but only a trail of blood showed where it had dragged itself into the forest.

He wondered then what his mother had learned since he'd been gone.

A month later, while he was still cutting bush, his mother came to him. She stood before him, looking at him but saying nothing. Mail came slowly and it was six months before a letter arrived from his father saying his mother had fallen from her horse and died of her injuries. "She walks," he said. She was a *draugur*, restless, frightening people in the district. They saw her everywhere and everywhere they saw her some harm came to them. The parishioners wouldn't let Einar bury Runa in hallowed ground. They thought that would stop the harm she did to them. When burying Runa in unhallowed ground had no effect and the accidents and illness continued, the parishioners asked the priest to help, but he refused. He said a soul buried outside sanctified ground was beyond his powers.

No one would come to the farm for fear of Runa's ghost. If Einar wanted to see anyone, he had to travel to the neighbouring farms, and even then, the farmers were wary of letting him through the door, because they feared his wife would come in with him. If a cow died, if a sheep fell over a cliff, if someone took ill, they blamed it on Runa's ghost. Soon, they turned angry faces to Einar because he had brought a witch from the Westfjords to their district.

When he had saved enough money, Sigurður built a house of lumber rather than logs. Because the town site turned to mud in the spring, he built a wooden sidewalk. When it was done, he walked to Winnipeg, then retraced his steps by train and boat until he was in Iceland at his father's door. He embraced the old man his father had become. Helga and the other two farm workers had died, so his father now lived alone. Sigurður bought two tickets on the next boat that took passengers.

He took his mother's dress out of her trunk. She had written that when he married, it was to be a wedding gift to his wife. He dug up his mother's bones, wrapped them in cloth and laid them carefully in her trunk.

When they arrived at his house in New Iceland, he carried his mother's wooden trunk up the sidewalk. He'd found no gold or palaces so he'd painted his sidewalk and house bright yellow. He carried the trunk into every room in the house. He showed his mother the furniture he'd built. The lace curtains he'd hung. When she had seen everything, he set the trunk on a kitchen chair. There were three china cups and plates on the table. He and his father sipped coffee from saucers while they clenched *molasykur*, hard cubed sugar, between their teeth.

The next morning he carried the trunk to the gravesite on the west edge of Gimli, and there he and his father buried his mother's bones.

SHLANDY

After the smallpox and the floods, many Icelanders left New Iceland and moved to the Dakotas. That is when the men in sheepskin coats came to settle west of Gimli. They brought with them their wives, women whose heads were covered in babushkas. Dark-skinned, dark-eyed women with shy smiles.

These new immigrants disappeared into the marshes west of town. They waded through swamps up to their waists. They built their white-washed houses on gravel ridges. Others came. The immigration agent tried to get these new settlers to go to the open prairie, to good land, land without stones, without trees. "You will break your backs on the stones," he said. "You won't eat bread there." But there were already some Ukrainians settled west of Gimli, and blood follows blood.

They came on Kristjanssons' boat. That was the beginning. Already the future was foretold. They went to the immigration hall west of the Betel Home. They called Gimli *Gimliyja* and the Icelanders *Shlandy*.

They used sickles to cut hay and thatched their roofs. They brought seeds with them and grew beans, beets, cabbage, corn, and cucumbers. Times were hard. They were made harder by corrupt government officials who made them pay for land that should have been free. When their wives worked in the city, their employers often refused to give them their wages.

One of them, Miskew, said to his wife, "You have to make what people will buy." He made a copper kettle and built a still. His wife was angry with him. "What am I to do?" he asked. "I can get no price for our grain. I can feed our grain to the pig or I can make whiskey."

He had spent the winter cutting firewood but his land had mostly poplar. Unless it was dried for a year, the buyers wanted a cord and a quarter to make up for shrinkage.

"It is not right to make whiskey," she said. She was a woman who took the priest *holopchi* every Sunday. "No good can come of this."

"Even the priest likes a drink," he replied. "What do you want for Mary? That she should go to school without shoes?"

Mary was their one child. They had lost two others and, for a long time, thought they would have no more. Then, when other people were beginning to have grandchildren, a miracle happened and Mary was born.

She was, her father thought, the most beautiful of all the young girls he saw at the weddings. When she was dressed in her embroidered skirt and blouse, when she danced the *kolymaka*, her beauty could have broken any man's heart.

It is nothing to have a beautiful daughter. Many men have beautiful daughters. Mary was gentle-natured, undemanding, clever at school, and industrious. When she was only ten she saw that other women in the community were often searching for good dill and garlic to make pickles. She took over a piece of her parents' garden. Her dill grew high and her garlic plump and firm. By the time she was in high school, women came from far and wide to buy her garlic. The money she made she gave to her parents.

Miskew lived not so far from town. Word spread that good whiskey could be bought at his place. The Icelanders liked to drink. They would appear in the yard with an empty bottle in their pocket and he would fill it up. Often, especially if there was more than one of them, they would stay to talk. In summer, they sat in his summer kitchen, in winter, in his house kitchen. Sometimes they would be hungry. His wife was an excellent cook. Miskew told his wife to make money feeding them roast pork, but they did not want vegetables. They waved them away, saying they did not eat grass. She learned to feed them sweet buns and cakes.

When his wife complained that what he was doing was against the law, Miskew would reply, "It is like a restaurant. What is wrong with a restaurant?"

He kept his homebrew in glass gallon jars and hid them in the swamp. He had to be careful, not just for the North-West Mounted Police but for customers who would come to buy while their friends would stay hidden in the bush, watching to see where he went to get the whiskey. "Do you want Mary to have a wedding and feed the guests stones?" Miskew said.

He showed her the jar in which he was keeping the money he made. He looked forward to the day they would have a wedding. They had only one child. He would pay the priest well. They would build a dance platform. He would hire the best musicians. Everyone would come. They would eat and drink for three days. Everyone would see that even though times had been hard and he'd had to work digging peat and building railroad beds, even though his crops had sometimes failed, he could still make a wedding as good as anyone.

"It is not so bad," he said. "They are Shlandy. What are they to us?."

The Icelanders came often, especially after the fishermen returned from summer fishing.

The second summer of Miskew's new business a group came and in this group there was a young man, Petur Solmundsson. He was loose-boned and blond and when the others argued and even fought among themselves, he sat and listened. He smiled a lot and was so shy he often looked to the side or at the ground. He smiled at Miskew, he smiled at Annie, but he would not look at Mary. When she came from working in the garden, or to bring something to put on the table, he blushed and looked away. He never came by himself, but always with a group of three or four fishermen. He paid for his whiskey and then sat listening to the discussions and arguments. When everyone else left, he left with them.

Young men began to come to court Mary. There was Woroba, Turkevich, and Leskiw. All good men. When they married, they would leave their parents' farm and buy a farm of their own.

"There is no hurry," Miskew said. "It is not like we cannot feed her. Besides, it is best to wait for a good offer."

In the time between going to bed and falling asleep, Miskew thought of the money in the glass jar. There was enough now for a wedding he would not have to be ashamed of and a little for a dowry. Mary would not be a beggar like her mother, pushed into her husband's arms because there were too many children and not enough food. He remembered that. All he had was a strong back and all she had were her clothes.

He did not like to think how he and Annie had lived at first. Now, things were better. They had a cow and every spring she had a calf. Once, she had two. Annie kept chickens and a large garden. She worked hard and knew how to take care of money. She was a good mother. She had taught Mary well. To sew, to cook, to keep a garden.

Everyone came to Mary for garlic and dill. Mary would give him grandchildren to make up for the children he did not have. Others had done better, of course. There was no denying that. He saw what they had. A dozen cows. They sold their butter and cream. They had good wood that was easy to sell. Their land was better. He had tested his land before taking it, digging a hole here and there and seeing the black soil. How was he to know that there were strips of good soil, then strips of gravel and stone that would dull a plough with one pass?

Already, in his head, he had planned everything for the future. When he fell asleep, he dreamt of Mary in her wedding dress. In the background a *cymbali* was playing. He did not hear the *cymbali* the day Mary did not return from school.

Annie was making *holopchi* and needed help, so it was a surprise that Mary did not come home right away. She liked sitting at the kitchen talking to her mother as they filled the cabbage leaves and rolled them into tight little packages. When Mary was half an hour late, her mother began to look out the window.

Her father stopped splitting wood and walked to the main road. He looked back at the house. His wife's face was pressed against the glass. After an hour, he walked into town. He stopped at the school but the doors were locked. He walked downtown and looked in the stores but they were all closed.

Everyone had gone home to supper. He knocked on Melowsky's door. Mary was friends with their daughter, Solemya. "Have you seen my Mary?" he asked. She shook her head.

He went to the teacher's house. The teacher was surprised to see him and asked if Mary was feeling better. "Is she ill?" Miskew asked. The teacher said he didn't know but she was not in class that day and since she never missed class, even on the coldest winter's day, he assumed she must be ill.

"Not in class," Miskew said. Fear made his bones tremble. "But where could she be?" He walked up and down the streets. He searched both sides of the road that led to his house. He knew she was not at home yet because his wife was watching out the window.

When he came into the house, his wife handed him a note. It was written in English. He looked at it, then gave it back to his wife.

"You read it," he said.

"I have gone to get married. Please forgive me," she choked out.

"What? Impossible," he said. "I have objected to no one. Even the one-armed Zubrak." He thought about the jar and rushed to get it. The money was still there in a tight roll.

"Shlandy," his wife said. "She's marrying Shlandy."

"Who? How?" He took the note and stared at it as if staring would change the words, make them more reasonable. "Shlandy? She ran away with Shlandy? Impossible."

"The young man who is so shy he always looks at the floor," she said. "The one who always came to sit in our kitchen. Your best customer."

He laughed. "It cannot be. They never spoke."

She said nothing. This was worse than if she had argued, had reasoned with him. Her silence meant that nothing could be done.

"I'll kill him," he said. "I will go to his parents' place and kill them both."

"They are not there. They took the train to Winnipeg."

"You knew!" he shouted. "You helped them."

"No. I knew nothing. Nettie came when you were away. She saw Mary at the train station. He was with her. She thought I should know. Now, everyone will know. You know what your sister is like. She will tell everyone."

"These Shlandy use magic," he said. "I've heard them talk about it. Invisible people. They cast spells with a magic language. She would not go unless he used magic. The priest will help to undo it."

"He would not have been here if you weren't selling homebrew. They would not have looked at each other. Are you blind? Did you not see how he blushed when Mary came into the room? Mary, you were always saying, give them some poppyseed cake. Mary, get them some perogies. 'They are good customers,'" she said, imitating him. "You liked having a pretty daughter to attract customers."

"You did not tell me."

"What would you have said to me? Don't be foolish. This *Shlandy* always pays and never asks for credit. He never makes trouble. You would have counted the money he has spent. Often he left his glass half-full. He didn't come to drink. The ones who came to drink licked the bottom of their glasses with their tongues."

"I will find them," he said, but already the sound of *cymbali* was fading, the wedding platform disintegrating, the musicians falling silent. "Mary," he said, his eyes filling with tears. He held his head in his hands. "Everything. I did everything for her." Then he laughed a sour laugh, "It is impossible. Who will marry them? No priest. The Shlandy is Lutheran."

His wife felt sorry for him, she thought to say through her own breaking heart, that she had warned him, that no good would come of what he was doing, that there is a price to pay for everything, that the devil lurks in every corner listening and waiting.

He struck the table with his fist. "No one. No one will marry them."

"His priest will," she replied.

He stopped, stared at her as if trying to understand what she had said. "No. That's no marriage. In the church with our priest, that's a marriage."

For many days he sat and did nothing. He refused to answer the door. He went into the bush and took an axe to his still. He broke the jars that were hidden in the swamp. He gave money to the church. It did no good. When he woke in the mornings, Mary wasn't there. When he went into town to buy goods at the stores, he felt as if everyone was laughing behind his back. The Ukrainians, the Shlandy, the Poles, the Germans. Laughing at him and all the times he'd described what a wedding he would give.

He asked his best friends why it happened. Why? Why? No one had any answer. "Was it so much to ask, to be a good father, to give his daughter a wedding of which she could be proud?" he asked his sister, Nettie. She glared at him but did not reply.

Finally, when he knew that nothing could be done, he went into his garden and spent part of every day tending his daughter's garlic. He took such good care of the garlic that it grew like never before, plump and sweet. No one else could grow garlic like this. His neighbours said it was because he watered them with his tears.

THE TROLL WIFE

A young couple named Sveinn and Elva lived just north of Gimli. Sveinn was both a fisherman and a farmer. Their land that fronted the lake was low-lying and in spring it often flooded. Here, the shorefront was thick with willow. Because the land close to the shore was so low, he'd had to build their shanty in a dense tangle of trees and bush further back where the land was higher. He'd been clearing his land for two years with an axe and a handsaw, then prying out the roots with an iron bar. It was a poor place but all the best ground had been taken by the time he and Elva arrived from Iceland.

One fall there were terrible storms and no fisherman could go onto the lake for a number of days. When Sveinn went to his nets, they were not where he had left them. The storm and the current had dragged them away, torn some of them loose from their buoy poles, heaping some of them on the shore, while Sveinn had to search for others with grappling hooks. He could ill afford to lose his nets and his lines.

When he hauled the nets to the surface, they were hopelessly tangled. He brought the nets to shore and worked the fresh fish loose. These he filleted and packed in ice. He hoped to sell or trade the fillets for things that they needed. The farmers to the west and south always wanted fish. Sometimes they had money but, when they didn't, they were happy to trade chickens, eggs, and vegetables.

Before Sveinn left, he said, "Elva, you'll have to spread these nets. I need to get them back into the water as soon as possible."

He had driven a spike into each of two adjacent trees and hung the first net across the space between them. His wife looked at the nets in dismay, because not only were the snarls tightly wound around the twigs and dirt, but around rotting fish. The smell was thick and oily and made her gag.

Elva shook loose some parts of the net her husband had started but then stood helpless before it. Beside her were piled more tangled nets. She sat on a rock and held her head and thought, "How can it be that this is my fate? If only I were beautiful, I could have any man I desired and he could give me everything I desire. I would give my soul to be beautiful."

That evening, after the sun had set, there was a knock at her door. When she opened it, an old woman dressed in black stood there. She said she had walked a long way and was thirsty and asked if she might have something to drink. Elva went into the house and came back with a glass of whey. The woman said she was tired and asked if it would be all right if she sat a while. Elva immediately agreed, for visitors seldom came her way.

"I saw the nets left by the storm. You have a difficult task ahead of you," the visitor said. "My name is Ragnheiður. Would you like my help? I am quick at this work."

Elva was pleased with the offer of help and readily agreed. It seemed odd to spread nets at night but there was a full moon and the reflection off the lake lightened the darkness. Ragnheiður did have deft hands. The twists and knots and snarls fell open as she touched them.

"If I had a husband who was more successful, he'd have men working for him who would do these chores." Elva said it with some bitterness because she had expected more of marriage. "I thought when we came to Ameríka that we would live like the elves. Our houses would be full of light. We'd have good clothes and there'd be plenty to eat and drink. I thought we'd all be cheerful, but the Icelanders here are as gloomy as in Iceland. No one was allowed to dance there and, here, even though the ministers now have no power, there is time for nothing but work."

"You have a husband," the visitor said. "You are fortunate. Your husband is young. He will live a long time."

"He'll never make anything of this land. It is nothing but trees and bush. We should move to the city. He can get work there."

She looked around at the dark forest. In Iceland there were no trees, but here there were trees everywhere, blocking the horizon in all directions. In Iceland, it had been possible to see vast distances from the farm, to see the mountains. "These trees feel like the bars of a prison."

"The land, as it goes west, is higher and not so wet. When he drains it, will it not be good land for hay fields and grain?" As she talked, Ragnheiður continued to work. She pulled deftly at sticks and dirt, dropping them to the ground, and then teasing the knots, twisting them one way, then another until they fell loose.

Elva would rather have talked than worked. She was eager to hear news. "Have you come from the city? Tell me about it. I've only seen Toronto from the train and been in Winnipeg for a day when we were coming to New Iceland."

Ragnheiður studied her, and then said, "In the city there are a lot of people living close together. Some good. Some bad. There are many places for working men to drink."

"Don't people wear fine clothes and go to entertainments?"

"Yes. But the work is as hard there as it is here. Many men cut wood all day. Others dig ditches." Ragnheiður had seen the Icelandic men who lived on the flats in Winnipeg in shanties. They often carried a saw and sawhorse on their backs, going from house to house, asking if they could cut wood. They were always searching for work, often taking jobs that gave them nothing but a place to stay and food. Some went to cut trees in winter and she'd heard about the hardship of working in deep snow.

"But some men are rich. They have fine carriages and large homes. They have servants to look after them."

"Does your husband want other women?" Ragnheiður asked.

Elva shook her head. "I married him because he would have me and no other man wanted me. When you are not beautiful, you have few choices. He is not handsome and no woman wanted him. Some think he is as ugly as a troll. He has a hunchback."

It was true that Sveinn's back was not straight. As a child, he'd had an accident and one shoulder was lower than the other and his legs were not the same length. He did not limp but it gave him an odd rolling walk.

"Is he lazy?"

Elva shook her head again. "He works hard but I want to live in the city. I want to wear fine clothes. When I walk into a room, I want men's eyes to follow me."

"Some men thought I was beautiful when I was young," Ragnheiður said. "It did not bring me happiness."

"It is what you make of it," Elva replied.

"Is your husband kind?"

"He never mistreats me," Elva said but her eyes were distant, watching some faraway scene instead of the small farmhouse and forest. In Iceland, she had heard people in Canada were wealthy, that they lived in fine houses, that everyone in the cities was rich.

As they talked, the nets which had seemed impossible to unravel were hung one by one from a crossbar, ready to be set. Just as they were finished, Sveinn arrived. Elva explained that Ragnheiður had helped her. Sveinn thanked Ragnheiður and said, "It is late. All we have is coffee and cream and some *skyr* but if that will satisfy you, Elva will prepare it."

Ragnheiður nodded and they went to the shanty. The living area had a table and two chairs, a stove, and some shelves with some books along one wall. The door to the bedroom was covered by a piece of cloth.

Sveinn said, "I'd offer you something for helping my wife but I have no money. I can give you some hardfish." He took some dried fish that was hanging from a string, and wrapped it in a piece of sacking. As he handed it to her, he said, "You've come a long way."

"I walked many miles in Iceland," Ragnheiður replied. "The deserts and the heaths are hard places and there were many doors closed to me. But that is past. Here, it is not so difficult. You have poor land on the shore," she said, abruptly changing the subject, "but behind, the land looks more promising. You could have a hay field there."

"Yes," Sveinn said. "I've dug some drainage ditches. The topsoil is many feet deep. Before I came here, I did not know such soil existed. The poplar trees are not so difficult to remove. It's the spruce that cause problems because of their size. Further back where you cannot see from here, we have some natural meadow and a small creek. The grass grows high. The water from the lake is good for drinking."

Ragnheiður got up to go.

"Will you not stay until it is light?" Sveinn asked. "The path is difficult for some distance."

"It is nothing like the paths through the mountains. There is no quicksand here and no rivers to carry you away," Ragnheiður responded, and he had to agree. Each year at fishing season, he'd walked for three days to get to the coast to work at the cod fishery at Vík. Before he left, he always said a prayer that he might arrive safely.

"I'll walk a little way with you," he said. "I'll help you past the worst of it." He turned to his wife. "Here," he said, "I brought something for your hair." He took out a length of green ribbon.

As they walked, Ragnheiður said, "Would you have given her the ribbon even if the nets had not been done?

"Yes. Life is hard here and she longs for better things. I would like to give her a better life but it'll take time."

"Does she love you?"

"Not yet. But maybe in a little while when things are better."

As they were going to part, Ragnheiður said, "*Guðs friður veri með yður.*" Since they had only met, she used the more formal wish that God would remain with him. "Perhaps we will meet when I come back in the spring."

He kissed her, as was the proper tradition in saying goodbye, and answered "*Farðu í guðs friði.*" His wish that God would go with her was heartfelt because she had helped without any expectation of payment. She had, he thought, a good heart. If they'd had more room and food, he would have asked her to stay with them. Elva would have appreciated the company of another woman.

That fall was milder than the last. The potatoes had grown well. The nets seemed to catch more fish. The hay had grown tall and thick. There was enough for Sveinn and Elva's animals. The winter had many warm days with no wind.

When Sveinn was away in the spring, Ragnheiður returned one evening.

"There is more land cleared," Ragnheiður said to Elva. "It is a slow business with an axe and a mattock but soon enough you will have a meadow. In the meantime you can plant potatoes and turnips around the stumps. Some have good luck planting that way."

"Séra Jón says that I should be satisfied with what I have. He says that to everyone." Elva had spoken to the minister, hoping to obtain his help in convincing Sveinn to move to Winnipeg. She had told him that Sveinn, with his limp and his lopsided shoulder, would be better suited to work in an office. Sveinn's English was still not good but there were Icelanders in Winnipeg who had started businesses and could use someone quick with numbers to keep their books. Before he had left Iceland, that was one of the things that Sveinn had done for the owner of the farm where he lived.

"You are not any happier with your husband than when I was last here?" Ragnheiður asked.

"Does it look like I have new clothes?" She spun around with her arms held up. "Does it look like this shack has turned into a palace?"

"When I was here last, you said that you would give anything, even your soul, if you could just be beautiful."

"Yes," Elva replied. "Who would not? Do you think someone would want my poor soul? Do you think it is of much value?" She said it with some bitterness.

"I have no use for souls," Ragnheiður said. "I want your husband."

Elva laughed out loud. "What use have you for a husband?"

"You don't tie your hair back with his green ribbon."

"It would have been better if he could have afforded a dress and a hat and good shoes." The words were sharp as broken glass. "Here," she said, "if you think his green ribbon is so wonderful, you take it and him with it." She went to a box on the shelf, pulled out the green ribbon and threw it on the table.

After Elva's outburst, there was silence between them. Nothing had changed. The shanty was as it had been, a small place made of planks. The furniture was crafted by hand. Dried fish were strung along a piece of twine that ran the length of the room.

To avoid Ragnheiður's steady gaze, Elva looked down at her own hands and noticed they were pink and soft instead of brown and rough. Elva held her hands up to her face and turned them this way and that, then she stood up and went to the mirror in the other room.

"What has happened?" she cried.

"We made a bargain," Ragnheiður said. "In return for beauty, you said I could have your husband."

Elva went back to the mirror. She came back holding her face with both hands. "Am I beautiful?" she asked. "Is it really me?"

"Yes," Ragnheiður said, "but there is no place for you here anymore. You must leave. You have what you want. Let us hope you have happiness from it."

Elva put on her good dress, wrapped her few belongings in a shawl and left without a backward glance.

Ragnheiður set to work cleaning the house. When she had done that, she began to spin so she could weave. Each night she worked. Each day she left the house and did not appear again until the sun was down.

When Sveinn came home from working for wages, wool had been spun and knit into mittens, socks, and sweaters, but his wife was nowhere to be seen. There was cooked food on the stove.

The house was clean. Baskets had been woven from willow and also made from birchbark. They were filled with wool.

He put the things he'd bought with his wages onto the table. Flour, salt, coffee, and oats, along with two good plates and cups and cloth for a dress.

The door opened and Ragnheiður appeared. Sveinn stared at her in silence. She was carrying wadmal she'd made on a loom.

"You spin," he said. He picked up a pair of mittens. "And knit. These are finely done." He looked up. "Where is Elva?"

"She has gone," Ragnheiður answered, "to find happiness."

He was preparing for bed when Ragnheiður came into the room. Sveinn turned to her, wondering what she wanted.

"Sleep beside me three times and then I shall have something to say to you."

Sveinn thought it an odd request but he was dazed by the disappearance of his wife and the presence of Ragnheiður. He nodded. There was no other bed and, in Iceland, they thought nothing of all sleeping together, young and old, men and women. He lay in the darkness, trying to understand what had happened but, eventually, he fell asleep. During the night, he dreamt he was making love to Ragnheiður, but instead of being an old, bent woman, she was young and beautiful.

In the morning, before dawn, Ragnheiður woke him. "I'm going now. Don't ask where or seek for me. I'll return when the moon rises above the edge of the lake."

They shared a bed this way for three nights, and for three days she vanished before the sun rose. On the fourth morning, she woke Sveinn before sunrise. She sat up and he saw not an old, bent woman but the beautiful woman about whom he had dreamt.

"Will I do for a wife?" she asked him. "In Iceland I was cursed to be an old woman before my time and a night troll. I was driven into the mountains. I know more than many and those who know more are feared. I was beautiful and many envied me. You have let me share your bed for three nights so the curse is no more. Will you have me or will you say no, and I will go unloved into the sunlight and turn to stone?"

"Will you love me with my bent back and my limp?" he asked. "Some say I look like a troll."

"I have your ribbon and I wear it." She showed him she had used it to tie back her red hair.

Elva did not go far before she met a man with a carriage and, like many men, he valued beauty before all else and, although he was married, he quickly offered her a ride.

In the city, another man took her in but she soon tired of him and, from him, she went to another. Her transformation had not changed her personality, and no matter what was given to her, she was never satisfied. There was always some man who she thought might give her more.

She had children but, since they were a burden that interfered in her quest for happiness, she fostered them to anyone who would have them.

People gossiped over coffee about Elva leaving for the city and a new woman, Ragnheiður, living with Sveinn. At first they were scandalized, but then they saw how happy Sveinn was and the gossip subsided.

Sveinn and Ragnheiður expanded the garden. They added on to the stable. They cut and raked hay. They worked as one and things went well. Little by little, as they grew in happiness, Ragnheiður grew even more beautiful, because she had come as a shape-shifter able to show her feelings in her face.

Hjálmar was a strong man, broad in the shoulders from rowing as a crew member on an eight-oared boat. The fishing ground beside where he lived was poor. There were few fish and those the fishermen caught were small.

Hjálmar, like the others, rented a house and land from a local farmer. The house, if it could be called a house, was not much more than a hovel, the sort of burrow in which one would expect an animal to live. The land was supposed to be enough to feed one cow, but it seldom was adequate because the good, level land was taken by the farm owner. Hjálmar's land, and the land of the other cottars, lay on a slope where the soil was poor and the grass grew thinly. They all paid their rent by cutting hay for the farm owner during the haying season.

The land the cottars rented would not support them. They had no choice but to make an arrangement with the farm owner to use his fish boat. In return, he took a share of the fish. His was an eight-oared boat but it held fifteen men. Six of those men plus Hjálmar lived on the farmer's land. The other men came from farms inland. They were sent by farm owners to fish during the winter season because there was not enough work for them once the hay was cut and stored. Poorer farmers from small inland farms often came with their hired men and servants because they could not afford to buy fish heads. The boat the farm owner provided was in no better repair than the houses he rented out. It had been pegged together with wood rather than being built with nails. If the wood were allowed to dry out, there was danger of the boat leaking faster than it could be bailed or even falling apart. As well, some of the wood was old and weak and should have been replaced. Many boats like it had foundered in bad weather.

Hjálmar's waterproof fishing clothes were made of sheepskins rubbed with fish oil. These were poor enough, but sometimes there were so few fish he could not afford to purchase new sheepskins and had to go to sea in nothing but his woollen clothes.

Hjálmar's crew members who came from inland farms lived in roughly made fishing booths close to the shore. Because of the distance to the fishing grounds, the booths were built on exposed beach rather than in protected bays. As poor as the turf house was where Hjálmar lived, it was still better than the fishing booths that housed the men sent from the farms. Their bunks were made of flat stones covered with sand. In an attempt to make the beds more comfortable, dried seaweed was piled on top of the sand. The crew often went to sea with nothing to eat and took nothing with them except whey to drink.

There were no jetties or piers. This meant that every day, the boat had to be launched through heavy surf. The entire crew ended up soaked to the knees and spent the day wet, in a North Atlantic wind, often in freezing temperatures, tending their lines.

The fishermen fished day after day, good weather and bad, but caught little more fish than was needed for their families to live. Because he was single, Hjálmar's share of the catch gave him food for himself and, sometimes, enough fish to carry two miles to the Danish store to trade for rye flour, rice, coffee, a few lumps of rock sugar, and some snuff.

Hjálmar's one luxury in life was his bay horse, Freyja. At fourteen hands, Freyja was larger than most of the Icelandic horses in the area.

She was stocky and strong. Because no grass from the home field could be spared for her, she led as hard a life as her master. When there was low tide, Freyja was often seen on the seashore eating seaweed with the sheep. At other times, she disappeared as she searched the bogs behind the beach. She lived wild year-round, except when Hjálmar was hired as a local guide by visiting foreigners, when he needed her to take him into the mountains on errands, or when she was needed to pull driftwood logs from the surf. When Hjlamar was pulling driftwood ashore for his landlord, he took the small pieces of wood allowed to cottars and carved highly decorated *askar,* the wooden bowls from which a person ate every meal.

When someone was needed to go an on errand to a distant farm, Hjlamar always volunteered. Others would not go because of the quaking bogs, the quicksand, and bad weather, but most of all because of the danger of fording rivers. On these trips, he took two more horses paid for by those who hired him. One extra to ride and one to carry supplies. When he travelled over lava fields and heaths, he sometimes needed a fourth horse to carry hay.

Hjálmar was hired because he was a wild man. He was the kind of person who, in spite of his poverty, liked to go further up the mountain than the sheep went just so he could see what lay beyond. He made maps and notes of where a river might be forded, where grass might be found, where there was good water. When he travelled the heaths and the swans were moulting and could not fly, he caught the young ones and wrung their necks. Their meat was tender. The meat of the older swans was tough but he ate it anyway. He skinned the swans carefully because the skins brought a good price.

"A wild man and a wild horse," his neighbours said. It was true. Even poverty and hunger had not tamed him. Freyja and he were a good match. No man could get close to her except Hjálmar. Yet, as wild as she was, she'd always come when he whistled. In return, he brought her grass whenever he could, even if it were only a handful.

Although he was only thirty-five, he was stooped because he'd been rowing since he was twelve. His blond hair hung to his shoulders and his beard lay well down his chest. When times were bad, Hjálmar, like his horse, ate seaweed. He ate it raw with butter or boiled in milk.

Everyone, even the farm owner, was a little afraid of him. The farm owner did not like Hjálmar but kept him as foreman because Hjálmar knew better than anyone where fish might be found. Once on the water, he knew when to be careful and when to take chances. Hjálmar, although he could have married, lived to himself, unwilling to bring children into a world where the farm owner compared himself to Napoleon and treated his tenants as little more than slaves, where the Icelandic employees of the Danish merchant cheated everyone and treated them with contempt. The farm owner often had been heard saying to his employees not to concern themselves with the cottars or the men who came to fish during the winter. It cost money to repair a boat, he said, but if a peasant died, it cost nothing to replace him.

At times Hjálmar went into the mountains to collect Icelandic moss and bring it back in bags. He shared it with his crew. When he was caught in storms on these expeditions, he took shelter in lava tube caves. He knew which caves were dry and which, even in summer, had openings filled with snow. He knew where the water was good and where it was bad. He knew where, if he were crossing the desert, there were small islands of grass. Sometimes, when he returned from his travels, he brought back trout or salmon and, a few times, when his crew members and their families had so little that they were softening sheep bones in fermented whey so the bones could be eaten, he brought back meat. When he did this, he waited until nightfall to return, slipping from house to house in the dark giving a share to each of the cottars in his crew.

"You should have a family," one of his crew once said, teasing him.

"The children die," he replied, and it was true. Few survived beyond their first year. It was not as bad as the Westman Islands, where every child died of tetanus. Here, at Snaefellsnes, some children survived to adulthood. "And, if I had sons, do you think they would go to Hólar and Copenhagen to study and come back and marry some rich farmer's daughter?"

"It's a terrible thing to be a thief," the pastor preached one Sunday. As Hjálmar and his neighbours walked home afterward, Hjálmar said, "Do you think he meant that lesson for the Danish merchant?"

A few nights later one of his crew came and said, "The *sýslumaður* is going to charge you with stealing sheep." The *sýslumaður* was the sheriff of the district. He was a brother-in-law to the farmer from whom Hjálmar rented his land. The farmer had started demanding he be given half of every halibut caught. It was against the law to demand this and Hjálmar had refused. Hjálmar had recited the law and the *sýslumaður* could not deny it, but as he was leaving, he said to Hjálmar that there was no place in Iceland for men like him, men who had no respect for their betters, no respect for tradition. Hjálmar had kept his halibut, but since then he'd waited for something to be done against him.

There was a sloop from Scotland in the harbour. The captain had finished buying horses and sheep and would sail in the morning. Along with the animals, he was also taking a small group of Icelandic emigrants as far as Scotland. From there, the emigrants would take a steamship to Quebec. Hjálmar knew there was no place in Iceland he could hide. From his trips in the mountains, he knew the legends of outlaws living on the heaths or in the lava caves were just legends. No man could survive there on what little there was to hunt or steal.

He rode Freyja into the countryside, then set her loose. They stood facing each other. "It's a hard life we'll both live," he said, "but if I sell you, you'll be cut up for shark bait and if I'm caught, I'll rot in prison. Go," he said, "go."

Hjálmar had some *rigs* dollars tucked away but it was not enough to pay his fare. His friends, remembering his late-night visits, loaned him what little they had.

He wondered who had betrayed him. He did not believe it was anyone in his crew. They'd faced death together most of their lives. There was no reason for any of them to tell the *sýslumaður* about his night visits but one of the landlord's servants who lived at the farmhouse might have asked a child what he'd eaten recently. The landlord's people kept close watch, always making certain the cottars took neither a piece of driftwood longer than an ell, nor a handful of grass from the farmer's home field.

Hjálmar cared nothing for the turf and stone hovel that he rented. The cow was not his. He also rented it from the farm owner. His belongings fit into a small, wooden trunk. He slung it onto his shoulder and his crew rowed him to the sloop at anchor in the bay. He asked the captain if he could work his way to Ameríka. The captain, short of hands, said he was only going as far as Scotland but Hjálmar could work his way that far as a deck hand. From there he'd have to pay for a passage to Canada.

When Hjálmar disembarked in Scotland, he joined the small group of Icelandic emigrants who had come on the sloop. With his savings and the money loaned him by the crew members of his fishing boat, he paid his fare to Quebec and, from there, to Winnipeg.

In Winnipeg, he found construction work, then went to New Iceland and stayed with Helgi Bjarnason's family. He worked that first fishing season with Helgi to pay for his board and room. He walked back to Winnipeg and found a job in a mill, then he worked in construction. He used his wages to build himself a shanty just north of Birkines and, with what was left, he built a flat-bottomed skiff. After that, he fished by himself and took jobs wherever he could find them. Men said many of the jobs were hard work but they weren't as hard as rowing an open boat on the North Sea.

Everything in his life had changed. No farmer came to take a share of the fish for the use of his boat, and more fish for the use of his nets, and more fish just because he wanted them. When Hjálmar went to buy something he needed, he wasn't treated with contempt because he had little to spend.

The hardest change was that none of his crew had come with him. He lived in a community of Icelandic immigrants but none with whom he had worked day after day, year after year. No one shared his memories. Still, he reminded himself when he was homesick, his shanty, although it was small, was better than the place he had left.

On the east side of his shanty, there was a small window that faced the lake. It was only one pane of glass but in Iceland, he'd had no glass window, only a piece of sheep's intestine stretched over a hole to let in a little light. He now had a chair, a table, a bed, and a good oil lamp. The floor was of wood instead of damp earth. He had a tin stove. The stove was, to him, like a miracle. In Iceland there was only one farm he knew of with a stove. Even in the farm owners' houses, there had just been a hole in the floor where people could burn dried peat and sheep dung.

In New Iceland, other settlers had taught him to cut down trees. He'd cut his own firewood and stacked it on the north side to shelter his shanty from the wind. He had wheat flour and butter and cream. He had a bag of rice and another of potatoes. There was plug tobacco and snuff on the shelf. He had moose meat frozen outside in a wooden box. In Iceland, he'd eaten meat once or twice a year.

He often thought of Freyja. If he had had her with him, in winter she could have pulled a sleigh loaded with his equipment and brought back his catch. Together, they could have travelled further from shore than he could go himself. As it was, he had to haul everything on a toboggan. Some fishermen who had made a little money had horses. Others had sleighs and teams of dogs. Freyja, he thought, would have outdone all of them.

After he'd been in New Iceland for two years, he received a letter saying the boat he had fished from had sunk and the crew had all drowned. The six cottars had been married. Six widows and their children were now paupers or would soon be.

With their husbands dead, there was no one to bring fish for their daily meals, no one to take fish to the Danish merchants to trade for grain and rice, for a piece of cloth for clothes, for a needle and thread. The mothers and children would be sent to separate farms.

Hjálmar remembered when his father had drowned. His mother had been forced to go back to the *sýsla* where she was born. Hjálmar and his two brothers and a sister were all sent to different farms. There was no mercy. No farmer wanted the trouble of keeping paupers. Hjálmar had never seen his mother or siblings again. He'd heard his older brother and his sister had died of diphtheria. His mother had died of something but he didn't know what. His younger brother, Lúðvík, he believed, was still alive. When Hjálmar had guided travellers, at every farm where they lodged, he asked after Lúðvík. Now that Hjálmar was in New Iceland, he dreamed of bringing Lúðvík to join him.

He'd been lost in thought. It happened sometimes when he should have been knitting himself mittens or socks or when he should have been carving an *askur* he could send to Winnipeg to sell. The people in Winnipeg didn't need wooden bowls to eat from, but they sometimes bought them as decorations. He had always liked to work with wood but there had been few opportunities in Iceland. For now, he would fish, because that is what he knew, but he was already thinking that he might become a carpenter and then a cabinet-maker. There were new opportunities.

He opened the door and looked out. The snow had quit drifting over the ice. If the weather stayed calm, it would be safe to go to his nets. It was hard for him to predict what the weather would do. He knew all the weather signs in Iceland but they were no use here. In Iceland, he'd watched one of the waterfalls that dropped from a cliff onto the shore. If the water fell straight down, the fishermen went to sea. If the water blew into the air like spray, they stayed on shore. Those times when there was no food left, they went to sea even when the waterfall turned to spray. On days like that, when they had passed through the surf and stopped to pray to God to protect them, they prayed harder than usual.

Even the storms in New Iceland were different from what he was used to. There had never been cold like this in Iceland, never the high drifts of snow and water frozen as much as six feet thick.

He put another piece of wood in the stove. He kept a pile of wood in one corner so that it would thaw and dry. He looked at the wood, split pieces of birch and spruce and poplar. He'd never had such wood before he left Iceland. In Iceland the only large wood was driftwood and the farmer owned the right to that as he owned the right to everything. The rafters of the house Hjálmar had rented were made from the ribs of a whale. The farmer even owned the bones on the shore.

He dressed, then got his toboggan from where it stood upright in the snow and collected boxes and equipment. He studied the clouds. They hung low, waves of grey to the horizon. The snow squeaked under his feet. The cold was intense but he was warm because he wore a moosehide jacket. He'd traded fish to a Cree woman for the jacket.

Hjálmar had been telling a group of men that one of the Cree had taught him how to snare and skin rabbits. They looked at his jacket and one of them said, "You are going native."

He'd shrugged. The Indians had been good to him. They invited him to go with them when they went hunting. When he had fish to trade, they were generous with what they offered him in return.

It was so still that he could hear the toboggan as it ran over the snow. There was no sun but that was good because there was no reflection to hurt his eyes. During the last few weeks, there'd been no fish in close to shore so he had twice moved his nets further out. He ran for an hour before he reached the small spruce trees he'd set up to mark his nets. He cleared the holes in the ice, then began to lift.

The catch was good, much better than he expected. He pulled the fish free and threw them onto the toboggan. They froze even as they thrashed about.

He felt the wind begin again, looked up and saw snow starting to trail over the surface. He hesitated, wondering if he should stop taking fish from the net and reset it, or if he should keep lifting the nets.

He thought about the widows in Iceland and how desperate they would be to get the little money that their husbands had loaned him. He was sending everything he could. They all had children. No one could survive on one cow, Icelandic moss, and seaweed. They would be desperate not to be declared paupers. They would lose all their rights and until they repaid the *sýsla* any money paid for their keep, they would have no rights.

He pulled on the net, dragging it up as quickly as he could, but the number of fish slowed him. Perch and pickerel, sunfish, jackfish. He'd learned the names of the Canadian fish. The wind began to gust, not from any one direction, but from one side, then another, sudden claps of wind that drove the loose snow before it. Then the snow started falling. Large, thick flakes. He went back to the far hole and pulled the net under. By then, the wind was blowing more steadily, not stopping but only dropping for a moment before rising again.

The shore had disappeared. He walked in the direction he thought was correct but after a time thought he must have started to circle. He couldn't tell by looking back because his footsteps were filling in behind him. If the wind had been steady from any direction, he could have used that to guide him. A steady north wind on his right shoulder would mean that he was travelling west toward land. But the wind blew first one way, then another. He wished now that he'd been able to afford a compass.

He squatted as he tried to remember his directions. Even as he rested, snow piled around his feet and onto the toboggan. He started to walk again, counting in his head so he'd know how long he had been walking. He had three chances of being wrong and only one of being right. The far shore to the east was twenty English miles away and had no shelter. He walked a long time and the drifting snow exhausted him.

He came to a pressure ridge. The blocks of ice rose higher than his head. He felt his way along it until he came to a place where the broken ice formed a shallow cave. He crouched there, out of the wind.

He wished that something he had learned in Iceland would be of use to him. To come all the way to New Iceland and a new life and then die of cold on the ice seemed not right. The injustice of it made him angry. Hjálmar thought of how the farm owner would laugh. He'd go about telling everyone that it proved he was right, that no one should leave Iceland for Ameríka.

Before Hjálmar fled Iceland, he and the crew members had talked about immigrating to Ameríka. When word had spread about their conversations, the farm owner had been enraged. He wanted no one to leave. Ameríka, he'd said, was too dangerous, too unknown, too far away. Some crew members had agreed with him but their death was already awaiting them in a leaky boat with rotten wood the farm owner wouldn't replace.

Luck, the vikings thought, was as much a part of a man's destiny as intelligence or strength. When Hjálmar received the letter from Iceland saying that his crew had drowned, he'd thought the *sýslumaður* saying he would arrest him for stealing sheep had turned out to be a stroke of luck. His luck had been with him. Now, he wondered if it had left him. Your fate followed you, it was said. Not even coming to New Iceland, it appeared, would be enough to save him.

The wind whipped against him. Snow gathered around his moccasins and in the fringe on his jacket.

"Freyja," he said aloud and, in spite of the stiffness of his face in the cold, he whistled for her. Many times in Iceland when he was lost in fog and snow, he'd let her have her head, held her by her tail, and she'd led him to safety through bogs and over fields of broken lava.

Now, she appeared out of the snow, looking at him as she often did when he called her. She made no noise but when he didn't move, she shook her head impatiently. She turned and began to move away. He stood up and followed her.

They walked for a long time. Sometimes, he stumbled on rough ice, sometimes his feet slid out from under him and he fell. At last, he felt stones beneath his feet. He bumped into his upturned boat that was buried under the snow, then the corner of the woodpile. He stopped, at last, exhausted, before his shanty.

Freyja stood, watching him, not moving. Frost was thick on her mane and on her broad forehead. If he weren't so exhausted, he'd have rubbed her forehead with his knuckles. She always liked that.

"Inside," he said, opening the door.

"Inside," he repeated. "Where it's warm." In Iceland when the weather was at its worst, he'd sometimes taken her inside.

He leaned on the doorframe. She started to turn away. "No," he said. "Wait. Stay." But it did no good. She faded into the falling snow.

He left the toboggan outside and stumbled through the door. The snow would cover the boxes of fish. In the morning, he could retrieve his catch. He took off his moccasins and knocked the snow from them, then shrugged off his jacket. There were still coals in the stove. He put on pieces of birch bark and then added pieces of wood.

He sat on his one chair and rested. In a little while he put water on the stove to make coffee and, with it, a pot of bean soup. He cut a thick slice of rye bread and spread it thickly with butter. As he stirred the soup, his mouth watered at the thought of eating the piece of fat salt pork he'd cooked with the beans.

The wind whistled under the eaves and raged around the corners. His shanty shook with the force of the wind.

He looked around. It isn't much, he thought, but I'm warm, I'm dry and I haven't been hungry in a long time. When his soup and coffee were ready, he took his Bible down from the shelf. Its cover was soft with age and its pages worn with use.

He dunked his bread into the soup and he would have said thanks to God for the food but, instead, the prayer that came to mind was the one the fishermen said every day after they'd launched their boat:

Í nafni guðs, föður, sonar
og heilags anda.
Almáttugi guð, ég þakka þér...

He tried to think of the words in English. "In the name of God, Father, Son, and Holy Ghost, Almighty God, I thank you," but his English failed him. He'd said this prayer from his first day as a twelve-year-old boy on board an open fishing boat. He hadn't forgotten his crew. He'd sent letters back to Iceland. He'd told them that as soon as he had the money to pay for their passages, he'd send it to them. He only needed to write to one person. His letters had been passed around, not just among the members of his crew but from farm to farm. There were many farm workers who, if they could raise enough money for their passage, would come to New Iceland. Some of them wrote back saying if they could raise the money, they would come.

As he automatically recited the words, the faces of the men he had fished with for years in Iceland drifted through his mind. All dead. It seemed unreasonable. Impossible. He knew how every man walked, how he caught his fish, how he rowed, how he reacted to a good catch and a poor one. They'd been thrown together by poverty and necessity. Few of them had anything but wives and children. It didn't cost anything to have children. No one paid much attention to the children until they were at least a year old. Too many of them died before then. There wasn't even much use in giving them a name until they were a year old. He didn't want to think about the children. They always ran down to the beach to help with the fish. He pushed the thought away because thinking about the children made him remember running to the shore to help with the fish when his father's boat came to shore.

Hjálmar had been like brothers with three of his crew. They all had been about the same age when they'd started fishing.

"God our Father," they had all said together after they'd launched their boat,

Son, and Holy Spirit, grant our blessing upon land and people,
Young men and old,
Cargo and ship,
Course and helm,
Thwart and deck, oars and bail out pail,
As well as all our rigging;
May our Lord's will be done, may we return safely,
And reach the shore of our choosing.

The prayer had worked for a long time and then, one day, it had stopped working.

Some of their bodies would have washed ashore. He didn't know which ones. Mail took a long time to come from Iceland to New Iceland. Someone would eventually write and tell him whose graves were on land and whose bones would remain in the sea. Many times, he'd helped gather bodies from the surf. What had happened was nothing new.

WHAT THE BEAR SAID

"Bless this food and bless them all," he said aloud. "Father, Son, and Holy Ghost, be good to them for they have suffered and be good to their wives and children for their way will be hard. Amen."

GLOSSARY OF ICELANDIC
AND FOREIGN TERMS

Ameríka: America was not a geographic place but a dream. The actual geographic and political divisions were unknown. When people said they were going to Ameríka, they were talking about a direction, not the United States of America.

askur: wooden bowls used for eating all meals

ástarbollur: round balls of deep-fried dough, they look much like Timbits

Black School: a school owned by the devil. There were no teachers. The students learned from books with flaming letters. The devil only appeared on the last day to seize the last student who left the school.

cimbali (tsymbaly:) Ukrainian hammered dulcimer

draugur: a restless ghost with magical powers

ell: about half a yard (same as *alin*), a measurement from the elbow to the end of the middle finger

fylgja: a supernatural being that is always with an individual. They sometimes are thought to precede a person and there are people who are sensitive to *fylgjur* and may say something like, "Uncle Helgi is coming. Put on the coffee," and Uncle Helgi does turn up. They've sensed his *fylgja*.

góða nótt: Good night, but also the title of a song often sung at funerals in Canada.

Gráskinna: magical manuscript in both Roman letters and runes. Its spells are powerful and often used for evil.

Grýla: a terrifying troll-woman who lives in the mountains. A law had to be passed to stop people in Iceland from using the threat of Grýla to scare children.

hangikjöt: smoked meat. On festive occasions the meat is most often a smoked leg of lamb.

Hólar: a bishopric created in 1106. It survived for seven centuries and had a school attached to it for centuries. Young men were sent to the school to be educated beyond the home schooling available in Iceland. The school has many legends about it and was, at one time, regarded with some suspicion for housing evil knowledge.

holopchi: Ukrainian cabbage rolls

huldufólk: invisible people similar to humans but who had magical powers which humans did not have. They generously rewarded those who helped them and fiercely punished those who harmed or betrayed them.

húsmenn: people who rented property on the farm owners land but did not make hay or use the pasture

Íslendingadagurinn: an annual celebration held on the first Monday in August to celebrate one's Icelandic heritage

jökull (plural *jöklar*): a glacier

kleinur (singular *kleina*): bowtie-shaped or twisted donuts

molasykur: hard sugar cubes, often sucked on with coffee

mysuostur: a brown or caramel-coloured cheese made from whey

pabbi: daddy

pönnukökur: thin pancakes like a crepe, often rolled with brown or white sugar

rétt: annual sheep roundup

rímur (singular *ríma*): a ballad often of great length written in four-line stanzas *rigs* dollars: small silver coins, Danish currency in Iceland. The value varied but was worth as little as thirty cents at some times.

rúllupylsa: a sausage made from boned lamb flanks, tightly rolled with spices and onion, boiled, then sliced thin and served on brown bread

Sæmundur the Wise (Sæmundur Fróði): a priest with great powers who, in many folk tales, tricks the devil. His statue is in front of the university in Reykjavík, riding a seal. He learned black magic so well at the Black School in Paris that he outsmarted the devil.

sætsúpa: a sweet fruit soup

Séra: reverend, religious title

Skálholt: the bishop's seat in the south of Iceland (Hólar was in the north). For eight centuries, this was one of the most important places in Iceland. It was a political and religious centre. Iceland's first official school, Skálholtsskóli, was founded at Skálholt in 1056 to educate clergy.

skuggabaldur: in popular tales a mysterious animal, a hybrid of a cat and a fox. They were considered to be particularly vicious in attacking sheep.

sýra: fermented whey

sýslumaður: the sheriff for a *sýsla* or municipality

uppvakningur: a spirit that has been conjured up to perform some service for the person doing the conjuring.

vínarterta: a prune torte, usually seven layers, probably the most recognizable symbol of Icelandic culture in North America. In Iceland they were three to four layers with rhubarb jam between the layers.

vinnumaður (singular): a farm worker.

ACKNOWLEDGEMENTS

I'd like to offer my thanks to all the people who, over the years, have told me stories. These have been my father and mother, both wonderful storytellers, the many people who drank coffee at their kitchen table and shared their stories to both tears and laughter. Thanks to Janis O. Magnusson for letting me read some pages of her grandfather's diary, for reading through the manuscript, to Atli Ásmundsson for helping me with the prayers in "Freyja," for lending me books and for putting me in touch with people in Iceland who could answer my many questions, David Arnason for thinking the few, first stories would be the beginning of a book and sending the ms. to Turnstone. It is impossible, after all these years, to remember accurately who told what story or part of a story. There were many stories about the large sturgeon in Lake Winnipeg, many stories of relatives who disappeared and reappeared, leaving and re-entering their local lives, many, many stories about the pain of leaving Iceland and the hardships that ensued. Small communities before the advent of television entertained themselves. Everyone was a performer. Stories were told and re-told, sometimes by the same person, sometimes by a number of people, each giving it his or her own twist. If I were to credit everyone who contributed to the stories in this book, the list would be longer than the manuscript. John and Kae Keller for a non-Icelandic view of us. Big Einar and Aunty Vi Einarson, Snooky Bristow, storyteller extraordinaire, Geordie Simundson from Pine Dock, Aunty Florence Fowler, Grandma Bristow (Gottskálkdóttir), Gunnur Isfeld, Lauga Magnusson, at 94 teaching me about *fylgjas*. There are the many stories in *Lögberg-Heimskringla* that are crammed with details of Icelandic folklore. Jim and Dennis Anderson with their stories of Libau and the marsh. Nina Colwill for her editorial advice and encouragement. To all of you out there who have told stories of Lake Winnipeg and, particularly, of the area called New Iceland, I hope I´ve done you proud.